HAPPY
MOTHER'S DAY

Yvonne Jack

GOTHAM BOOKS

Gotham Books

30 N Gould St.
Ste. 20820, Sheridan, WY 82801
https://gothambooksinc.com/

Phone: 1 (307) 464-7800

Published by Gotham Books (August 16, 2022)

ISBN: 978-1-956349-38-2 (sc)
ISBN: 978-1-956349-39-9 (e)

Dedication

I dedicate this book to my **Mother**.

&

Special thanks to
M.Mikail *Gorbachev* Geoffroy
for typing this manuscript.

Acknowledgement

In acknowledgement to my elementary school teacher **Ms. Clement**, who once said to the 12-year-old, "Yvonne Jack you can become a great writer one day." Still waiting (smile)

In acknowledgement to Miss H and some of her young art students of Medgar Evers Preparatory College, for helping to bring forth my vision for the cover of this book.

Table of Contents

For now, the coming storm has been pushed to the back of her mind – Ma Jo Jo is in a state of euphoria. She has travelled back into the distant past, way, way, way back... She is this young girl Josephine, once again...

Soon the stage will be hers, all hers but for now, she's enjoying the bacchanalia, that's swirling around her, enjoying the antics of the six young women, the village's lovable hussies, who have been tasked with producing but not invited to participate in the actual fashion show, no, definitely not!

They, the six young women on becoming aware of the restlessness of the early arrivals, have decided to take matters into their own hands and bring some levity into the seemingly charged room, by entertaining those early birds, to a free fashion show, an impromptu one, the likes of which they'll never see again.

The hilarity of these young women, stumbling and tripping over their own feet, in their most likely borrowed thimble and stacked heeled shoes. Some of them clutching at the front of their blouses, which could not be buttoned up or groping their exposed backs. Their clothing, like the shoes was likely borrowed from the makeshift closets that were prepared for the '*real*' models. The slim young professionals, coming in from the city, to take part in the gala that is being dedicated to the young Josephine, who will be embarking on her singing career in Brooklyn, New York!

The crowd is in stitches, doubling over in uncontrollable laughter because the young women have mockingly taken over the personas of professional city models, with their expressionless or nonchalant faces. These antics, along with their stumbling, entices more raucous laughter, stomping of feet and even tears rolling down the cheeks of some of the attendees – it is well known that none of these young women, are of that bent, expressionless or nonchalant.

Finally, the long-awaited show begins and Josephine who in addition to her budding singing career, holds the secret ambition of being a fashion designer one day, is awestruck, as she watches the professional models twirl, sashay and curtsy in front of the huge appreciative crowd.

She is enthralled by the colors and designs – Yes, those seemingly intricate cuts that are being displayed on stage. The Fish Tail, The Slingshot, The Shift or sack dresses as some call them! The too – tight hobble skirts that have been paired with the peasant or off-the-shoulder blouses – The style of the moment – This style that's preferred by the most daring or *'out there'* women. Those gathered waisted or pleated skirts and dresses are definitely not for them, but for the sedate and demure women; Frankly, those church – going women.

The stage, now cleared of all the *swishing and swooshing* of fabrics and exaggerated stomping of feet by the *so-called* models, now belongs to the young Josephine. The stage, her moment in the sun has arrived. She is going to perform her medley of Josephine Baker and Sarah Vaughn songs for this huge adoring crowd.

Possibly this whole village and attendees from villages near and far have turned out to hear her final local performance. It has been rumored that she is going to New York to record an album, the first for her or any other villager! Even babies in arms have been brought here by wistful mothers, some of whom may have suffered unfulfilled dreams, so definitely would not be missing out on this performance for anything in the world.

The elderly and infirmed too, who have decided not to miss out on this performance have hobbled out of their homes, on their 'crook stick', their makeshift canes. Their eyes glistened with hopeful tears for their fellow villager. They are now seated upfront on the few chairs and benches - borrowed from the village school.

'Their Josephine', is going to the great and mighty U.S.A, Brooklyn New York to be precise. Besides *cutting* this album she will be embarking on a glorious and successful tour as promised by Mr. Leo. Then, soon the village, the country; the world will hear the melodious voice of Josephine Charles! Her voice according to some, comparable to Josephine Baker, *better than*! Others would indignantly interject.

Happy that electricity was now had throughout the village and pleased that they will be able to hear the beautiful voice of *their* girl loud and clear, most of the villagers vowed that even before the album comes out, they'd be ditching their crackling transistor radios, and signing up for the services that the *'radio fusion people'* were offering. Yet still, some will be going into the city, to *pay down*, Yes, put a deposit on a radiogram, now available in the big stores. Yes, they will be able to play her album, along with the 'Hottest' Calypso records that they will be purchasing.

~~~

The young Josephine Charles, waiting patiently in the wings, knows that the audience must be craning their necks – the women more so, anxious to catch a glimpse of her beautiful dress. Brought from the 'States' by Mr. Leo. The young Josephine finally makes her appearance. She's hearing the oohhs and the aahh's from the female sect, the wolf whistles and appreciative comments from the males. She is giddy with all this adulation. She looks down at her beautiful dress, Mr. Leo has delivered indeed! Whispering in her ear, he had let on that there were even more beautiful ones to come her way. Those paired with beautiful shoes or purses and jewelry too! Then the Young Josephine, had squirmed until he released, the tight hold in which he held her, his hands slowly falling away from her shoulders, lingering a bit too long, on her lower back.

Josephine is called forward and drifts towards the *mike*, which is handed to her by the M-C. "Take it away – Take it away", the woman with a smile, encourages her to start the song. The young Josephine does not hear her; she's looking downward, her eyes transfixed on her dress. The intense and artful handiwork; she's taken in by the intriguing work done with the beautiful beads and stones against the shimmery black satin; just as she would have done it herself; and if she had seen it, Ma Z would have agreed that it was indeed a beautiful **'*dan dan*'**, the dress. As if in a different world, Josephine Charles decides to take a stab at another aspect of this glamorous life – she's about to embark on, the modeling side of it. Yes, she too has just become a model! She glides, sashays, dips and pirouettes, along the length and breadth of the stage. Josephine has the crowd on its feet, the deafening claps, and roars of approval, are encouraging as she twirls and twirls
~~~

Chapter 1

With eyes closed, Ma JoJo twirls right into a piece of furniture; it is her *Wagonette* that holds all her fine and seldom – used dishes and drinking glasses. Her meeting with the furniture is painful, as her arthritic left knee, absorbs the full brunt of that contact. Her tear-filled bleary eyes connect with a newspaper photograph encased in a crudely handmade frame, standing inconspicuously between her prized wine glasses on one of its wooden shelves. With trembling fingers, she opens the glass door, of that most treasured piece of furniture, with its delicate wooden trimmings and moldings – A present from Pa Joe Joe's 'sainted' grandma. A *tyrant*, if you were to ask Ma Jo Jo. 'A very kind and generous woman'. Pa Joe Joe would have shot back forcefully, she, having gifted this house to him.

Ma Jo Jo snorts, because she knows that this so-called generosity was not extended to her, that she was just a byproduct. She was quite aware that the grandmother along with the rest of the village had long branded her with the scarlet letter. Steeped in the belief that she had destroyed Joseph Celestine, their great white hope, who through his athletic prowess was destined one day to put their village on the map, ridding it of its distasteful status, of being *'behind God's back'*, a backwater village and its people being called *Country Boukies.*

Ma Jo Jo smiles wryly at the thought of those enlightened town and city people who thought thusly of the village and its people, yet sneaking in a steady stream, as much as three times a week, seeking spiritual and medicinal help from its faith healers and again, derisively called *Bush Doctors*, for their herbal medicines, bush baths and the like, to heal whatever their hifalutin city doctors could not heal.

Ma Jo Jo now allows her thoughts of the village and its people to drift to Pa Joe Joe and questions, why didn't he leave her alone, let her stay out of his life, as the villagers wanted all those years ago. Was he punishing her, since theirs was no life lived?

Ma Jo Jo snorts again, as she recalls the grandmother; standing right there in the village square accusing her of being a fallen woman and a blight on her grandson, before Pa Joe Joe demanded that she shut *her* **trap**, and that he was going to marry his Josephine, with or without her, his only living relative, blessings.

In the thickening cloud, that's fogging up her psyche, Ma Jo Jo carefully navigates her fingers, through the dust, cobwebs and rarely used wine and brandy glasses, intending to pluck the photograph from its unenviable place way behind the precious glassware in the wagonette, hiding perhaps? Trance like, Ma Jo Jo is swaying and twisting in front of the open doors of the furniture.

Its inviting, daring her to put her hand in its fiery mouth, to pluck the forbidden photograph out its roiling belly – to dredge up the ugly past, in which she was a victim too.

Ma Jo Jo is clueless that she is being unwittingly pulled into the past, a place that she should not be right now, not with the coming storm ...

~~~

Now the excited crowd falls dead silent, holding their collective breaths. Their Josephine has at last sauntered back to the microphone and is about to sing. After her last two stumbles across the stage, she knows that her foray into the modeling business is over. She has decided quite wisely, that this is not her **thing**. The audience is quiet but restless – this is the last time that they will be hearing the voice of Josephine, *their* girl, with the voice of a kiskadee, nightingale even. The next time they will be hearing her voice will be on a record – Not the same.
~~~

Suddenly the quiet hall has come alive, as the man of the moment, *no*, every moment in the village – the one who makes the village **happen**, steps onto the stage. The crowd gives him an appreciative hand clap. He, Mr. Leo, takes his place amongst the five-hat wearing and grim – faced women at the table, with its brightly colored plastic covering.

The young Josephine clears her throat – The crowd goes wild. They are anticipating the songs that she will be singing. Songs by Josephine Baker and Sarah Vaughn, her eyes are scanning the crowd. She is searching the crowd for the face to whom she will be rendering these songs too, her Joseph Celestine.

She sees him; she's wistfully looking at him. Her eyes wanting his to meet hers and see a deep love, the hope that hers hold. Sadly, his does not meet hers, his crestfallen face is turned toward the exit. She knows what this is all about – the man seated at the table amongst the hat wearing women. He has come back to the village, to take her away to America, where she would perform nightly at his club in Brooklyn. There, he keeps on saying with confidence, that she will surely be discovered, making tons of records, all number one hits, and become a famous star!

Even her mama, who once herself had dreams of becoming a big singing star, excitedly urged her to take the leap; that Mr. Leo would take care of everything, will see that her dreams come true, full stop! Whenever her mama talked that way, she was never sure if she was talking about her, or of her lost dreams, and what could've been.

Even her dreams of one day designing dresses, that she would go to the village seamstress, and drool over in the magazines – she will be able to do this in America! And yes, Joseph Celestine would eventually be alright with her decision to leave the village for America. And yes! He will eventually join her in Brooklyn, her mother will assure her half-heartedly, with lots of eye rolls.

At the *mike*, Josephine is rendering heartfelt song after heartfelt song to the sullen – faced Joseph Celestine, who in turn is not looking at her, punishing her for her decision to pursue her career in New York, essentially leaving him.

At the table, an angry Mr. Leo is observing the sad display by Josephine at the *mike* and the brutal brush off by the spiteful young man. Mr. Leo swears that being alone with him in New York, will make her forget that she had ever known such a 'spoiled child', a brat! He sighs, there would be those he will be leaving behind too, but he would make sure that they would never require anything. The woman won't be hurt, she has her church and her young son. He felt a sudden tugging at his heart strings, at the thought of the young boy. He paused for a moment in his thoughts, his hands flinching, as they are wont to do whenever he is harboring troublesome thoughts.

He sighs and exhales long and hard; No, he won't take him away from his mother. The young boy, only twelve years old, was a source of joy and had a stabilizing effect on his somewhat mentally fragile mother. Mr. Leo was utterly proud and boastful of his son, who already knew that he was going to be a psychiatrist like his uncle, Mr. Leo's brother in the U.K. and Mr. Leo often wondered if the boy's professional choice had anything to do with his mother.

~~~

Ma Jo Jo still swirling in the dense fog of her yesterdays, easily surrenders to her memories of her fellow villagers ... Suddenly, Josephine becomes distracted by a painful and guttural cry, coming from the table behind her. It is the soulful cry of regret, of loss, being retched out of the throat of one of the hat – wearing women, Miss Viola.

Looking at Josephine on stage has brought back painful memories of her sister Mimi. She too had left the village ten years ago with Mr. Leo for his club in Brooklyn, New York and his promises of making her a singing star, making records, and embarking on successful tours.

Soon Miss Viola was in New York for her sister's funeral, through the generosity of Mr. Leo, who bought her an airplane ticket, and looked after her lodgings, with one of his relatives. Without his help, she surely would have been lost, staying by herself in a hotel.
~~~

Miss Viola read and reread the favorable writeups about her sister, in one of the local newspapers in which Mr. Leo was a minor shareholder. Mimi had saved those newspapers in which she was featured, to send to her sister Viola, but never got around to doing so. Truth be told, Mimi was beginning to regret, having left the village, her safe haven. She had become a slave to too many people and *things* – she just wished that they would leave her alone.

Through Mimi, Mr. Leo lived his fantasies of managing and maybe bedding some famous singers – He even dressed her like some of them, his idols. Now, Mimi was no more, gone by her habitual deadly mix of drugs and alcohol. This he would never acknowledge, but Mimi's drug use was fueled by his constant sexual and mental attacks on her.

Re-reading the articles on her sister Mimi, Miss Viola would glow with pride. Then she would burst into torrents of tears, quickly musing that Mimi was not just being boastful in her letters about the adulation by the audience in Mr. Leo's club and interest in her, by some in the music industry, with whom Mr. Leo would forever be negotiating.

Her letters were earnest and breathless just as she was in person. Miss Viola could often see her and hear her in those letters – Yes, her excitable little sister. *"Viola soon I'm going to buy you a big house; a shiny new car and get you out of that backward village!"*

Miss Viola would giggle about the car; this was just a dream of her sister, because she never took to anything with wheels – Not even a bicycle! Oh, she was wrong, the box carts of her youth. Those wooden box carts sitting on prams or any other discarded wheels, were the village children vehicles, as they'd sit among the empty water vessels in the carts and raced each other to the streams and springs, their water sources from which they would fill the empty vessels.

Now, Miss Viola Wails again and even louder. She's wailing at her failure to grasp her little sister's cries for help. Mimi loved the village, she would never call it backward, she was hinting that she wanted to come back to it, to come back home! Miss Viola's series of fresh frustrated screeches, is now for the young girl Josephine at the front of the stage, looking more like a deer in the headlights, than someone who is about to experience unimaginable fame and fortune.

Miss Viola's frustrating screams are rending the air, stifling her fellow hat wearing women around the table. The young girl Josephine, is at the mercy of this *scamp and he* would surely destroy her as he did her happy go lucky and innocent sister, Mimi.

Ganja, Marijuana, this was something in which some youths in the village partook but this thing called Cocaine, was not in the village and she was sure that this *evil* was forced on her sister abroad.

Miss Viola is looking into the questioning eyes of the young Josephine, who has abruptly turned around at the sound of her screeches. Miss Viola is frantically fanning at the beads of perspiration that are just standing there on her forehead – The wide brimmed hat is not helping any. She lifts it off, revealing her bald pate, which surprisingly does not draw any reaction from the crowd. She quickly mops at the sweat before replacing the sweat stained hat.

Mr. Leo is intently looking at the young Josephine and ignoring the screeching woman who is standing over him. Miss Viola can't see his face, but she is sure that he is all eyes on the young girl and not in a *good way*. Once again, she focuses her eyes on young Josephine but its her Mimi who is standing there! Her eyes are pleading with her to get away from him, his friends, their drugs and alcohol!

Miss Viola has been transported back to that awful day and the frantic phone call ... She scampered up the hill to the Irish woman, the only house – holder in the village with a telephone. She had been summoned up the hill by the woman's servant, Elizabeth. Miss Viola knew it was not a good call through the bulging eyes and stammers of the woman, she, repeating over and over "Mimi! Mimi! Mimi!" Miss Viola then left poor Elizabeth in the dust, as she hauled up her skirt that was flapping behind her like some *mad bull* kite and raced up the hill to the Irish Woman's house.

Now, Miss Viola shakes her head furiously; she doesn't wish to continue with the memories. The *'comboside'* is striking up the music once again, Miss Viola is looking at young Josephine's perplexed smile – Miss Viola is mouthing the words "Run! Run! Run!" to her **'sister Mimi'**, because she wouldn't hear her impassioned pleas above the din of the musical instruments. The crowd is becoming restless and the catcalls are resounding all through the large hall. The delicate paper fan in Miss Viola's hand, has suddenly become weaponized and with all her might, she brings it down over and over on Mr. Leo's head.

Miss Viola does not wait to see the startled look on Mr. Leo's face, or hear the guffaws of the crowd as she angrily huffs off the stage, running out of the crowded room with the puzzled spectators crowding the doorway, quickly clearing the way for the now belligerent woman, the usually timid Miss Viola.

With bedlam reigning around her, the young Josephine turns back to the crowd, for the only one whom she thinks would help her make sense of this madness, but he too has disappeared, he is not there anymore.

The agitated M.C. gravitates toward Josephine and with a plastered-on smile, urges between gritted teeth, "take it away, take it away, take it away, darn you!" The young Josephine ignores her. "Take it away!" she snarls again to the unresponsive girl.

She knows just where he'll be, she's got to find him and fly straight into his arms to persuade him to see things her way – that everything will work out in the end. Before she flees the stage, Josephine becomes entrapped in a visor-like hold. She turns her head and Mr. Leo is standing behind her. She feels and smells his alcohol fueled breath on her neck. He draws her sharply into him, tightly clenching her waist as she feels his manhood boring into her. She's uncomfortable with all this, and tries to break free, but he won't allow her to do so. He is desperately stating his case, rapidly spouting his knowledge of the new life she would soon be involved in – The fame, the travel, the money but most of all his undying love for her. Using her elbow with brute force, she jabs him in the stomach, temporarily disabling him, jumps off the stage and flees the building.

The young Josephine is bathed in tears of confusion and fright, from the unwanted attention from the older man. Thankfully she is spared from seeing the emotive changes in his visage – disbelief, anger, determination, and the sadness as she runs out the door.

~~~

Just like her younger self, Ma Jo Jo is once again bathed in tears as she continues to relieve every aspect of her pathetic past … …

Mr. Leo plods back to the empty table – he plops down on the lone cane bottomed mahogany chair. That fine piece of furniture, was provided especially for him – the village's generous benefactor. Now he is sitting all alone, the women having beaten a hasty retreat amidst Miss Viola's most embarrassing wails yet.

Mr. Leo sighs and looks out onto the empty hall, empty and unbelievably silent as if none of the restless feet had been there, just minutes ago. The songs on the Sarah Vaughn L.P. that Josephine was supposed to be rendering, are playing on a nearby gramophone, that he has managed to crank up. He feels a twinge of sadness that's compounded with the guilt he now bears. He begins to look back on the not-too-distant past …

He had promised Miss Viola and meant every word of it; to take care of her sister Mimi, to make her the star that she so desperately wanted to become, but then she was taken in by the bright lights, those 'sharks' in their cheap suits, fedoras, Panama hats, two toned shoes, and the fat cigars, that they'd continually be chomping on.

Mimi was also a flirt who teased him to no end – then it was all over, when he started bedding her and in doing so gave her the upper hand to call the 'shots', he being helplessly in love, could not stop her from ruining what could've been. America with its bright lights and easy accessibility to everything addictive had gotten to her, as it had gotten to countless other young hopefuls, unprepared for the wild ride to fame. Mr. Leo feeling the knowing knot of discomfort in the pit of his stomach quickly reaches up and touches his forehead – yes, they were there alright, the beads of perspiration – the beads of fear.

He is reliving those past years all over again; he is looking at his young bride to be, the unsure smile on her face, scared maybe, as
~~~

she walked up the isle on her father's arm. Her gait slow and unsteady because of her very extended belly and he guessed at the time, the high heels that she insisted on wearing.

The closer she got to him the tighter the knot in his stomach became. What with her brothers and other relatives manning every door; every possible escape route of the church. He smiled inwardly since he had long chased away any thought of running away. At this time of his life he was not prepared for the *'proper cuttail'* that it was rumored throughout the village the relatives were prepared to give him.

Mr. Leo smiled tenderly at her – no, he did not love her, but he would do right by her and his boy that she was *'carrying'*, according to the village's midwife. He had his life to live, his plans did not include a family just yet, but he would do right by them. The relatives could put away whatever weapons they had, with which to register that beating on him.

Mr. Leo, now gets up from the table and stretches, the knot in his stomach had disappeared, so too, have the beads of perspiration on his forehead – he having sopped them up with his shirt sleeve. Now he wonders at the sudden reemergence of the knots of fear in his stomach after all these years. Deep down he knows it's his fear of not getting the young Josephine away from the young man, Joseph Celestine.

Once again back at his seat at the table, Mr. Leo studies the only other occupant in the room, the cleaner, the village's handyman, and the resident drunkard. He, busy at his task of rearranging the hall, now empty of its disappointed and rowdy occupants brought to near – riot stage, due to the nonperformance by their soon to be recording star and compounded by the fact that they could not make head nor tail of the earlier confusion on the stage.

The Cleaner is drenched in sweat as he stacks and repositions the chairs and tables. Now, having seen enough of the cleaner, *'Mr. Rumbo'* the name tragically affixed on him by the villagers because of his seemingly always drunk state. Mr. Leo unfurls his lanky frame and reaches yet again behind his chair for that *'bottle of babash'*, the illicit and undistilled liquor that he had been imbibing for quite some time. He gets up, stumbling along the stage, miraculously steadying himself before he reaches the edge and catapulting over.

Mr. Leo searches through his scrambled brain for the cleaner's birth name, not wanting to call him by the derogatory one affixed to him by most of the villagers. Being a bit intoxicated himself, the name escapes him. Through the dust clouds being raised by the man's frenetic and hurried sweeping motions, Mr. Leo blinks and calls out slurringly; "Aye dere, Aye dere, 'ello dere!'" He repeats his calls between hiccups as he stumbles, licking his lips and the bottle swaying in his hand.

He uncorks the bottle and takes yet another swig at its content – a reckless move, he, knowing quite well the potency of the liquor from the so-called distillery way above the waterfall, high up in the mountain, that is financed by him. Mr. Leo tries to focus his bleary eyes on the man and his frenetic movements, the *bushbroom* in his hands, coming apart. With a bit of cloth that he had acquired to tie the bushes that he had gathered by the riverside, he fashioned them as a broom, with the length of guava rod, his means of a broom handle. The bushes seem to be going their separate ways now, with every one of his frenetic movements.

Mr. Leo smilingly looks at the bits of bushes going every which way, as the infuriated man makes long sweeping motions in the hope of completing his task before the entire broom falls completely apart. He again backs away from the edge of the stage, plopping down on the middle of its bare flooring, the *bottle of babash* securely between his legs. '**The best in the business**', he was often complimented on the liquor that flows through the night club, that he owns locally and is managed by one of his wife's brothers.

Mr. Leo knows the cleaner did not hear him because he is focused on finishing the task at hand. The end result would be him collecting the few shillings, his pay and then, he repairing to the chineseman's shop where he would purchase two six cents loaves of bread and an ounce or two of cheese, which the chineseman would cut off from a big block, and weigh on his scale – but he was always generous with *Mr. Rumbo*, putting a dab or two of margarine on his bread – no additional cost!

Looking at the bent back of the hard-working man, Mr. Leo wonders at his and most of the villager's compliant nature and is suddenly awashed in sadness and guilt as he recollects his father's anxious face on his deathbed. Now, a procession of his ancestors flashes before him. He again draws the bottle from between his legs and takes a long swallow and another and yet another. He's rapidly blinking his eyes as he feels the liquor heating up, spreading throughout his chest, taking control of his tortured mind.

Mr. Leo does not care that a sudden burst of his agonizing screams has reached the ears of the *drunk* who drops the *bushbroom* and is approaching the stage at a surprisingly fast clip, to the aid of the seemingly distressed Mr. Leo.

Yes, Mr. Leo is anguished, somewhere along the way, he had broken the deathbed promise that he had made to his father to protect and look after the villagers whose ancestors, a disparate band of not quite a hundred, had left their island, along with him and his family, settling here in this little village, making it their new home.

Now he's quite embarrassed that he, with his guttural screams, had drawn the attention and concern of all people, the village drunkard, who is puzzled by his emotional state. Mr. Leo tosses him a scornful stare, that sears through his consciousness, reminding him of just who he is – the *village drunk*. Leaving the man muttering to himself as he picks up the scattered pieces of bushes, fashioning them yet into another broom in order to finish his job.

As is his custom, Mr. Leo takes a long drag from the unlit cigarette that he had placed between his quivering lips. This cigarette was pulled from the near – empty packet from his jacket pocket. He looks up at the imaginary smoke that he blew out, curling its way up into the ceilingless building. That he had proudly built – *financed*, he corrects himself, as he had done with other projects in the village. He not having driven a nail, lifted a bucket of sand or sawed off a piece of lumber, to which his father would have proudly approved, had he done so.

He feels his sensitive emotions rising; are they being propelled by these guilty feelings he now seems washed in? Mr. Leo throws his hand in the air, and questions frustratingly, "now what more do you want from me papa?" With the bottle in hand, he tries to stifle the self-hating drunken laughter emitting his mouth, but only succeeds in hitting himself in the face and tipping the bottle, some of its contents spilling onto the stage as his drunken laughter comes in bursts of fits and spurts.

They left him so much in cash and kind to look after their people. Immediately the images of his father, his uncles and their wives, waist deep in the muck of the swamp land, trying to save the cattle that had strayed too far in the swamp, or they leading herds of donkeys downhill, laden with baskets of fruits and root vegetables that vendors from nearby towns, would be coming to purchase for their weekend sales in their markets.

Mr. Leo hears and feels the rebuke of his ancestors, who are now flitting in and out of his drunken consciousness. Their denunciations of him, coming fast and furious. Piercing his soul, cutting at him, leaving his wounds wide open – their bitter words, like grains of salt sprinkled there on. There is no escape, Mr. Leo feels cornered, trapped. Now he sees her, the white-haired woman who never smiled, not even with him; even though loving him fiercely. The woman with the very large holes in her earlobes – the only one in the village with a nose ring, a round silver one. His friends were afraid of her, not being able to understand her dialect and thought her mad because of the way she laughed, no, cackled and dressed like no other in the village. Swathed in yards of colorful materials, oftentimes, the end of the material trailing behind her in the dust.

For all her quaint ways, the young child Leo, loved her dearly, especially when she would allow him, a ten year old boy, to sit on her comfortable laps – His head snuggled between her ample breasts, looking up into the face that shone down so much love on him. The thick lips from between which such melodious songs glided – the words of which he could not understand nor cared to. He only knew that he was in her arms and being lulled to sleep by the songs of this wonderful woman.

Mr. Leo blinks his bleary eyes at the apparition of the woman slowly disappearing, going back to the distant past from where she belongs; just as his other ancestors had just done. He bends and retrieves the cigarette that had fallen out from between his lips and goes back to the table where he begins to study the antics of the cleaner.

From the far corner of the room, the cleaner had seen the spillage on the stage and is licking his lips as if tasting some of the droplets of the illicit liquor. With the knowledge that he is nearing the end of his task, the cleaner's movements are becoming more frenetic – the movements with the broom quickening, causing the dust clouds to rise even higher. He is covered from the crown of his head, right down to the soles of his bare feet in the dust. Mr. Leo cannot discern the color, *much less* the patterns on his printed shirt. Just the unusually bright red of his tongue as it flicks in and out of his mouth and over what might be his very parched lips. Mr. Leo's vision is becoming very distorted by the dust clouds and his intake of an inordinate amount of liquor.

Peering keenly through the dust clouds, he does not see the cleaner anymore but there is this little girl smiling at him. For some reason the dust clouds are thickening even more, but the girl is still there – Though she's now a bit older. My gosh, she's the cleaner's daughter! Mr. Leo feels a sense of pride – through his influence and money, he had gotten her a place at the newly opened and only primary school in the village, then on passing her exams to a prestigious school in the city, he thought it only right to finance some of her daily needs too, especially her **'passage'** – her transport.

The dust finally settled and unsure of his next move, here stands the cleaner; all by himself. As the cleaner, Mr. Leo too is alone and angry. He lifts the bottle and uncorks it with his teeth, with some of the contents spilling down the front of his shirt – and he watches the liquid as it dissipates into the cotton fabric, thankfully it escapes the expensive jacket, bought in Brooklyn on Flatbush Avenue where he would shop for his *getups* – especially the two-toned shoes he loves.

With the thought of Brooklyn, the memories of Mimi comes back, rushing into his consciousness. The woman, Viola and her gut-wrenching screams are deafeningly resounding in his ears. Mr.

Leo shakes his head, hoping to keep the next thought from flooding his mind.

He knows that the majority of the villagers silently vented their feelings, blaming him for the popular Mimi's death – the village's hope for being recognized as not just another one *'behind God's back'*. Those that did not voice their opinion one way or another, only did so because of their feeling of indebtedness to him, his financial generosity to them personally, or to the village as a whole.

Mr. Leo sighs and shakes his head again, this time as if to clear it of the debilitating effects of the alcohol. Mimi was gone years from his life – he cannot or maybe does not want to remember how many years. He tries to lessen his guilty feelings, by recalling Mimi's brutality to him; even if it was fueled by drugs and alcohol, she often condescendingly reminding him that she was the conduit via her voice to the loves of his life – The, Josephine Baker's, Sarah Vaughn's and other voices continuously in his head.

Mr. Leo sighs and looks upward – the large *'carpenter nails'* piercing the galvanized sheetings, covering the ceilingless roof, look down at him as if to remind him that the job is incomplete. The evening sun refusing to slink away, is unmercifully beating down on the roof. Its heat generating noises scolding him for his laxity on covering same – it being six years since the completion of the structure its sitting on.

Miss Viola and her sister Mimi, just won't leave him alone. They're there hovering in his head. They surely must have known that despite her running roughshod over his heart, that he would have done and indeed had done everything within his power to save her, back in New York.

Mimi had emotionally left him the moment that she arrived there and saw the bright lights, took the stage in his club, sang her first song and heard the first of thunderous applause. Mimi knew that she had arrived, yes, and on her arrival, she simultaneously *'Flew the coop'* – left him.

"Aye dere, aye dere saga boy," Mr. Leo, now drunk and unsteady on his feet, calls after the cleaner. "Ketch dis saga boy," he calls again, carelessly twirling the bottle of liquor in his hand.

Immediately, the cleaner drops what is left of the *bushbroom*, and with his heart in his hands, sprints to the stage and in the nick of time catches the precious near empty bottle as it leaves Mr. Leo's limp hand.

Mr. Leo blinks rapidly and finds himself looking down into the face of the now disapproving high school girl of whom he is so proud. He smiles at her, but she does not return his smile. Her disapproving face begins to morph into that of her father's, the drunkard.

Mr. Leo, in his drunken fog is staring down into the grateful toothless smiling face of the father, who is bowing earnestly as one in prayer, earnestly thanking him over and over for the poison, the destroyer of lives, that he has just tossed to him.

"Get outta here! Get outta here!" Mr. Leo venomously spits out at the puzzled man. Then he immediately feels pained for the brutal words that he has showered on the poor helpless man, wishing that the words could be redirected, to him, who is really deserving of them.

He is miserable, he knows that this is all about the young Josephine who ran out on her performance, on him, in search of Joseph Celestine. He had fallen in love with her the moment he saw her on stage at the school concert, which he was invited to by the headmistress, his cousin, who knew just how much he sought after local talent. Yes, he had fallen head over heels for a fifteen-year-old girl.

He has waited all these years nurturing her career from afar and not to mention his love for her. Now, one way or another, he was going to get her away from that young man Joseph Celestine. His maturity, his worldliness and his sincerity would surely win her over – always did with those other wide-eyed village girls of whom he never took advantage.

Mr. Leo abruptly ceases his meandering thoughts and leaps off the stage, landing unsteadily on his feet and is steadied by the hand of the cleaner. He's overcome with an overpowering sense of compassion as he looks into the unsure eyes of the man who quickly almost apologetically removes his hands from off of his shoulders.

Mr. Leo wants to assure him that his kind gesture is appreciated and from henceforth he would take care of him just as he had taken care of his daughter, who had joined the rest of her siblings in removing themselves from him - their father, the village drunkard. Instead, he digs his hand in his pocket and retrieves a few shillings and drops them in the man's trembling outstretched hands, pats him on the head and flees the building stumbling along the way.

In spite of the sun blazing down, Mr. Leo feels the chill, so he stuffs his hands in his pants pockets. He's on his way to get his love Josephine away from the young man who could do nothing for her. Soon, they will be in Brooklyn NY, where she would gravitate from the small stage in his club, he is sure to bigger stages across the country. Yes, he would make her his star! Mr. Leo assures himself, that his Josephine will still secretly sing all the Sarah Vaughan and Josephine Baker songs to him.

Mr. Leo stops and deeply inhales the cool fresh air that's propelling the swaying bamboo and tall reeds by the riverbank to entangle each other. Because of his inebriated state, he trips and stumbles along the rocky tracks, he's feeling this sudden burst of anger and is trying to convince himself that this destructive emotion, has nothing to do with his thoughts of the young man for whom Josephine had fled the building but for his earlier thoughts of his father, and other ancestors whom he believes that he has failed.

Mr. Leo frees himself of his linen jacket, tossing it on the tops of some bushes as he continues his stumbles along the rocky tracks. This day is not conducive for jacket wearing; as a matter of fact, he has discovered that since living in Brooklyn NY and it changes in climate, that in this almost hot and stifling weather, no day is suitable for jacket wearing. He hopes that maybe some ambitious young man with an upcoming job interview for some high hifalutin firm in the city would be lucky enough to find the jacket.

Panting heavily, he bends over, his beltless pants down to his knees now and blinks away the perspiration from his eyes. The clear glass like skies gives nothing away. *Not one tiny floating cloud, a beautiful bird, not even a stinking corbeau? You don't hear what I say? OK I'll settle for a stinking buzzard then!* At this time down on his knees, his mind screams up at the unanswerable Sky. Mr. Leo's shoulders now shake with sickening laughter. Still, he gets no reply to his just completed screed. But wait! He is listening to the soft mournful cries coming from between the tall bushes ahead of him. His ears perk up, he straightens up and brimming with curiosity, hurries along to the whispered cries.

There ahead in the clearing is his Josephine! He will recognize that melodious voice anyway, even in unimaginable emotional pain - its Josephine's! Now something seems to be terribly wrong, she is not hitting the right notes. Her quivering voice is telling him that she needs him! Mr. Leo shakes his head in disgust whatever drama she is going through right now, has to be the fault of that young fool Joseph celestine. Mr. Leo is certain that their encounter had not gone the way that she had expected.

He collects himself, and hurries through the tall bushes, the blades of *Razor Grass* nonchalantly taking swipes at his face. Nothing matters to him now, but the welfare of his Josephine who needs him more than ever.

She collapses in his arms, the anguished sobs that's wracking her chest, is piercing his heart, shredding his very soul. Weak and totally spent from the rejection of Joseph, her love, her life, she cannot now fight him off, Mr. Leo drunkenly smothers her with what he perceives as compassionate assuring kisses. Josephine feels her heart and soul taking flight on her words, they are begging him for mercy as they compete with her ragged breaths, they trying to escape her soon to be useless body.

The excited and agitated Mr. Leo forces her to lie on the soft carpet of green grass, all the while cooing to and shushing her. She sees it in his eyes, that with his next act it was going to be all over – her world was going to be crushed completely.

Now the bloody rains come down, suddenly and harshly, just like the unimaginable pain that explodes in her body does too! Yes, just like the large blade that comes down suddenly on Mr. Leo's back over and over. The blood spurting upwards, then falling back down as rain; harshly and silently!

Chapter 2

Ma Jo Jo is at it again, her dancing. Her footwork is awkwardly fleeting, yet still fanciful. Her eyes are transfixed on the photograph in her extended hands, she being farsighted. Ma Jo Jo's dance movements have suddenly gone up a notch – have moved from being frenetic to almost volatile, making her arm gestures seem ragged as if trying to divorce those limbs from the rest of her body or maybe her arms from the forbidden photograph, that seems to glom onto her hands.

She stops suddenly and sheepishly looks around before settling down on one of her cane bottomed straight back chairs, just in front of the wagonette. Ma Jo Jo lifts her very flared skirt and mops her face from the sweat that's pouring down from beneath the tightly wound scarf on her head. There is this nostalgic smile playing at the corner of her mouth, which she quickly rids herself off. Her eyes are cloudy, and she is once again fixated on the photograph.

Ma Jo Jo, because of her bleary eyes, needs more lightning, so she gets up, bypassing the lamp with the soot filled shade and moves over to the flickering lamp with the words 'Home Sweet Home' printed on its clean shiny and fragile shade. Balefully, she looks at the photograph, while tracing its outline with her forefinger and only now realizes that it has been pierced with a sliver of broken glass. This had occurred when upon hearing the sudden rolling thunder and seeing the bright flashes of lightning, both of which she is deathly afraid, she quickly attempted to get the photograph out of the wagonette and succeeded in spilling and breaking some of her fine drinking glasses.

Ma Jo Jo ignores the blood and keeps on tracing the outline of the photograph, which represents the destruction of both their lives. Now, she abruptly ends her ruminations, gets up from the cane bottomed chair and on tippy toes circles the room, with some questionable dance moves. As if propelled by the dangerous winds outside, she is now back in front of the wagonette. Swaying, she replaces the photograph amongst the broken shards of glass, and makes as if she is dusting her hands, shaking it - ridding it of what it represents perhaps?

Ma Jo Jo winces and looks at her swollen finger now encased in her dry blood. She blanks her mind from the violent encounter with her fine wine and brandy glasses in getting to the innocent looking photograph.

At the top of her lungs, she begins to belt out her favorite Sarah Vaughn song. She is pleasantly surprised that she could still pull off the high notes. Ma Jo Jo is getting louder and louder, higher and higher! When was the last time had she opened her mouth to sing with such gay abandon?

Suddenly she pipes down - what must her immediate neighbors be thinking of her sudden gaiety with Pa Joe Joe gone, only two weeks? She grows glum and annoyed. She's thinking again of her missed opportunity - her supposed farewell concert so many years ago.

With what seems to be a vengeance, Ma Jo Jo starts the Sarah Vaughn Song all over again. Loud and superfluous, she is rendering this song to Miss Viola and her sister Mimi, on whose slender shoulders Miss Viola had placed such a heavy burden; succeeding in the music business for them both.

Miss Viola lived a very frugal life herself, every penny going to Mimi, music wise. Yes, by the '**hook and the crook**', "my Mimi is going to make it", she would voice this statement to herself to reinforce her belief in '*their*' success.

Ever since the choir mistress from the Anglican Church which they both attended, opined of Mimi succeeding as a recording artist if steered in the right direction, Miss Viola started doing just that, steering her there. If Mimi needed to travel more days to the city for her voice training, quite an expense, Miss Viola provided her **'passage'**, her money, anything to secure her success. *'They'* were going to be famous!

Miss Viola herself once held secret ambitions of becoming an actress just like Gina Lollobrigida or Marilyn Monroe. After all, she had all the starring roles in her school plays. Even though they mimicked, making fun of the villagers way of life. She gained praises, waves of applause, and multiple curtain calls.

Yes, she knew that the roles performed by her idols but never seen by her, were shown on the silver screens in cinemas miles away from the village, in places she had never been to in her youth.

Still, Miss Viola fiercely held onto her secret, by ferreting out the already read movie magazine from the piles that her boss, the wife of the newspaper publisher would leave for her to dispose of, ever so often. The day when the **madam** came into the servant's quarters and wordlessly handed her a movie magazine with Carmen Miranda prominently on its cover, Miss Viola became flushed with embarrassment. Was her secret out, was she being laughed at? In spite of herself Miss Viola felt her excitement rising. This one, Miss Carmen Miranda was just like her! Her dream really could come true!

~~~

Mo Jo Jo abruptly ends her rendition of the Sarah Vaughn song. She is listening to a series of thuds on her roof, and the screeches of the frightened birds being blown out of nests, their homes in the mango and avocado trees. She is sure that the fallen branches on her roof are those of the **'zaboca'** tree, whose limbs are seemingly the less sturdy of the trees that abound her yard.

It is early yet, the storm still hours away. She should not be frightened or alarmed by the premature arrival of some heavy winds. Now, really startled by the raucous sounds outside her closed board window, she peeps through it's cracks - she looks on wide eyed, as the window is being violently shaken. She has become aware that the window is being attacked by the angry birds with their beaks and wind assisted bodies, slamming into the window.
~~~

Are they trying to break in? What did she do to deserve this potentially calamitous and unwanted visit? Everyone knows what a visit by these vengeful birds portends.

Instinctively, Ma Jo Jo goes back to the living room for the photograph in the wagonette, knocking over the last of the standing wine glasses. Just as quickly she decides that the photograph is safer right there. Abruptly, she turns around, arms outstretched, her bulk blocking the glass door of the furniture. Those determined birds of vengeance would have to go through her to get to the photograph.

Ma Jo Jo is looking at the lone bird that has gotten in via the unfinished ceiling but has ended up stuck - trapped by one of the long-galvanized nails protruding from the roof. Now quite disturbed, she turns around and grabs for the photograph that's standing alone and vulnerable amongst the fallen glasses that had been crushed by her heavy hand.

She holds the photograph to her chest, it is lying protected on her breasts, under both her hands. No one or nothing is going to take away from her this cherished memento not even *him*, if he is trying to do so through the birds. This photograph represents the beginning of the end of her life.

Ma Jo Jo positions herself just under the dying storm bird, commanding it to drench her in its blood, to cleanse her with it and maybe then and only then, he, Pa Joe Joe would forgive her. She listens to the last squawk of the storm bird, sees the last attempt of a flutter from its trapped wings; see it's last droplet of blood as it falls on the *gazette* paper that she has hastily placed under it; Its neck pierced by a protruding nail. She looks up into the dying bird's glazed eyes and wonders; why does he hate me so?

She sits down on the cane bottomed chair in front of the wagonette. The birds atop her house are still with their eerie squawking. She wonders what her neighbour's thoughts were on seeing those riotous birds on her roof. The birds looking akin to storm troopers, as some peck away at the board windows and even at her front and back doors as if readying to launch an attack on her.

Ma Jo Jo begins to softly hum another of Sarah Vaughn's songs but this time her humming comes off, as a series of painful moans. She cannot now stop the disturbing memories from churning, belching up their toxicity as if from a disturbed volcano. One after another they are coming to the forefront, Ma Jo Jo is hissing and grunting ...

~~~

The crowd is growing restless and very vocal, despite the village's elders exhortations for calm. *Their boy*, Joseph Celestine is being brought to the courthouse – his trial begins today. A group of his friends are gathered in a tight circle, trying to keep one of their own under control. They are back again on the courthouse steps, after having been chased away for the umpteenth time, by the custodian of the small, quaint building.

The police standing nearby, *throw* their keen eyes over at the unusually large village crowd. They suspect that because of the personalities involved, spectators from other villages are in the mix.

One or two '**Bad Johns**', those bad boys from outside the village have infiltrated the group of friends and the police have found out. One in particular, was *fixing* for a fight with just about anyone. He is hoping to use this highly charged crowd to start a battle with the authorities; the police have gotten word of this.

The group that he really belongs too, is standing on the outskirts. They have stored their weapons of choice; bottles, stones and '**bullpistles**', those most feared weapons, made from the preserved penises of bulls – from those slaughtered bulls, which probably must have once grazed in the open fields across from the courthouse.

Again, '**One Man**', or '**Bag of Bones**', another of the names that he is sometimes referred, because of his very skinny frame, is called upon to stop with his '**gallerying**', his showing off. He had become the defacto leader of the group since their adored leader, Joseph Celestine has been in the lock up and standing trial today.
~~~

One Man is moving through the crowd with the new swagger and persona he had adopted since he began working on the wharf in the city with *'real men'*, as he would boastfully describe his days with those seasoned *wharfmen*, whenever the villagers tried to bring him down a peg or two.

One Man had gotten his wish; as a young boy whenever he accompanied his father on his *'run'* to the wharf where he would collect the provisions for the Chineseman's shop; He would often vow to become a wharfman one day.

He was impressed by the way they would fling *serious* cuss words, good naturedly at each other, their drinking and gambling as they waited their turn to offload the provisions from the just arrived boats coming in from the neighboring islands. Most of all he was impressed by the width of the leather belts around their waists, that made them seem like superhumans! He would daydream of the day when he too, on becoming a wharfman would dress and cuss good naturedly as they all seem to do.

Frequently, his daydreaming would end by him receiving a sharp thump on his back from his father. The father, himself a wharfman before being saved from such a hedonistic lifestyle, *her words*, by the young religious woman, who became his wife and Carlton's mother. The mother refusing to call her son by the nickname, *One Man* or any other foolish ones ascribed to him.

One Man, surveying the growing partisan crowd, begins to resort to empty threats of violence, especially threats of what he'd do to the magistrate, jury or anyone connected to the case if *'his boy'* was to be convicted and sentenced.

One Man hated to be ignored as is being done to him now. He digs his hands deep into the pockets of his dungaree pants – he is beltless at present. His one and only belt got broken earlier on, so his pants keep slipping off his waist. He digs a hand in his shirt pocket and retrieves a pin, the big safety pin that he always keeps on him for emergencies such as this.

He walks away from his group of friends, hauls up his shirt, draws the pants waist tighter and is about to secure it with a big safety pin, when he hears the titters. Embarrassed he looks across the yard, into the laughing eyes of the young ladies, teenagers all, whom from time to time he had tried to impress. He gives a big '*steups*', sucks his teeth loudly, as he would do when lost for words.

With the pants waist finally secured, One Man stands his shirt collar up, pulls out a crumpled kerchief from his pants front pocket, shakes it out and stuffs it into a back pocket, leaving the greater portion of the plaid 'kerchief, limply hanging out; this the fashion statement of the day amongst the '**Saga Boys**', the '*dude boys*'.

The snickers of the teenage girls turn into cries of horror, as once again, One Man digs into his pants waist and pulls out what looks like the handle of a dagger. With a satisfied smirk on his face he repositions it in his now tight waistband – it's silver handle of which he does not make too much of an effort to hide, popping out from under the front of the shirt that's missing a button or two.

Happy with the attention he has just garnered from the young women, One Man saunters back to rejoin his friends, who greet him with rebuke or disgusted shakes of their heads. They had seen or heard the terror in the girls screams, having been fooled by what they thought was a real weapon. *The weapon* peeping out from One Man's waist, was in fact just a replica of the real thing, skillfully made of wood. This most surely was acquired from a masquerader at the end of the just completed Carnival parade, in the streets of the city two weeks ago.

~~~

Now, the raucous noise coming from the neighbors next door has brought Ma Jo Jo out from what is now one of her too frequent forays into the past – her way of avoiding what's to come. The noise does not faze her, she knows that it's from Elvin's donkey, only it does not sound like its usual brays, in fact it does not sound like any type of braying.

Ma Jo Jo knows that the beast is scared by the thunder repetitively rolling and screaming across the heavens and the bright lights of the lightning sneaking into its stall at will today. Ma Jo Jo smiles knowing that Elvin would, if he thought that he could get away with it; bring the scared animal into his mother's home. With
~~~

that, she burst into hearty gales of laughter, her shoulders shaking uncontrollably, her hands on her belly as if to hold down the belly laughs. She sputters and coughs; the laughter coming even faster and louder as she pictures Elvin's parents in this imagined scenario; the mother standing at the front door blocking Elvin and his donkey's way onto her highly polished floor. She with the massive arms on her ample hips. Her angry eyes glowering, mouth twitching. His '**maga**', thin father, standing behind her large frame; somewhere he always seemed to be. Ma Jo Jo picturing the '*nashy*' man still behind his wife's back, rebuking his son for his actions, calling him a '**nincompoop**', equating him and his actions to that of the village's troublemakers. The wife quickly turning on him, berating him for even thinking of her loving son and One Man and his ilk with the same thoughts. Just recalling the person behind the name, One Man, has sent Ma Jo Jo back into the past from where she had emerged only a short while ago ...

~~~

Ma Z, yanks open the door of the awaiting taxi and flings herself on the front seat, "trouble! trouble! trouble!", she breathes to its two other occupants. She then relates what she has just heard; threats leveled at the law by certain young men, if their friend Joseph Celestine was convicted.

The young Josephine seated in the back seat, looks at the sweat pouring down from beneath Ma Z's black funeral hat. Josephine did not dare tell her anything, but she had frowned at the choice of her hat and its color, an old one from her vast collection of beautifully decorated hats. 'Today is not a day about fashion!', she would have chided Josephine whose suggestion she would normally listen to. Ma Z known for her great sense of fashion, dressed now in a simple black dress, hat and black shoes on her feet, just does not cut it today.

To be sure, Ma Z is conflicted and in emotional turmoil, in essence '*a ball of confusion*'. She really did not want to be a part of '*this*', did not want to be a part of the melee that is sure to take place later on. Even her best friend Selma, in whose husband's taxi she is presently sitting, had warned her about attending '*this show*' and had
~~~

refused **point blank** to accompany her, letting her know that she of all people would not be welcomed there.

Miss Selma knew that both parties involved were loved by the villagers and this bacchanal was causing unbelievable strife and friction and she was not about to choose one over the other, so she was definitely staying out of '**dat**'!

As she waited for, but on realizing that a reply would not be forthcoming to her common sense exhortation, Miss Selma huffed off and forbade her husband, a non-participant in this one sided conversation, from transporting Ma Z and '**dat one**', referring to young Josephine to the courthouse in '*my*' taxi. Whenever '*vexed*' with her husband, Miss Selma always claimed the taxi as her motor car, spitefully throwing it in his face that it was through the loan from her father, that he was able to make a down payment on the taxi.

Ma Z looks around at the charged crowd and feels a heavy pall bearing down on her. What did she do to her Josephine? What did she do to encourage the village to treat her this way? Just how many more referred to her as '**dat one**', she wonders in dismay? Wasn't it just yesterday that they all hoped, wanted her to become the local Sarah Vaughn or Josephine Baker? Those with electricity promising to flood their homes on weekends with her voice via the records on their just bought radiograms. Those without, had nothing to fear because the past- time on weekends in the neighborhood, were the playing of music at their loudest shaking the rafters and rattling the glassware in the wagonettes and '*safes.*'

My gosh, what did she do to her Josephine. Was she wrong in not wanting her to become just another village wife or like her, an unwed mother? Brooklyn New York was calling her Josephine; Mr. Leo had told her so!

This steely woman, her eyes with unshed tears turns to Josephine in the back seat lying under the flour bag made sheet, as she was ordered to. Ma Z awash in guilt, turns to her side, uncomfortably so, and offers her hand to her. Josephine refuses it, she was already following Ma Z's commands, though unwillingly so.

The taxi driver who is unobtrusively taking in all the *'going ons'*, on the outside as he is won't to do, nudges Ma Z with his elbow, alerting her that something of importance seems to be happening. The crowd has begun to converge around Mr. Brian the policeman, who has ridden up on his bicycle. This, Ma Z keenly takes in, craning and swiveling her neck towards the crowd, but not getting out of the taxi.

Mr. Brian is ignoring most of the *'fast ball'* questions being hurled at him except for those quietly and politely asked by the grimmed faced and somberly robed men and women who are respectfully given space and a wide berth upfront by the crowd. After giving his rapt attention to those preferred people, Mr. Brain with bicycle bells ringing impatiently, walks his way through the thick throng, and gets back on the bicycle, only when he reaches the gravel track and speeds off.

The crowd encircling the religious leaders are ready. As the sounds of the clanging brass bells, gleaming in the mid-morning sun rings out; the fidgeting feet and swaying bodies are in motion. Songs of praise, glory, power, and victory are pouring out of the hearts and souls, straight out of mouths of the believers. The voices, together with the thick black smoke from the burning incenses in the chalices are rising as high as the praises – hopefully going up to heaven, to the **FINAL JUDGE'S** ear. Victory! Victory! Victory! Belts out the believers.

Ma Z wonders, victory for whom? Out there, there are two separate camps competing for that victory. The youths are supporting Joseph Celestine, who they believe was driven to commit this so-called crime of passion in defending his Josephine. The act was horrific enough, leaving Mr. Leo in a coma for one month and hovering at deaths door for another two.

Then there's Mr. Leo's supporters; the older heads, the benefactors of his generosity to the village. Even the small courthouse in which this, the biggest case yet in the village was about to be held, is one of the many things, brought about by his financial backing or his agitation to his friends in *'high places'*, or directly to the agencies responsible. These older heads would close their eyes to what he has purported to have done; this man who continues to do good by the village, even though no longer living in the village and not a permanent resident in the country but in the good ole USA! They have to believe that Mr. Brain was attacked by the jealous young man, period!

It was felt, that for the good of all, the now absent Josephine should stay away from the court proceedings, remembering nothing about Mr. Leo's drunken attack on her or the brutal and gruesome one on him, by Joseph. Josephine true to form, remembered nothing, thus was of no use to the questioning authorities.

The air shattering noise of the excited crowd on the courthouse grounds fills up the small Vauxhall motor car, despite its closed-up windows. Ma Z, its sweating occupant, sees the crowd drawing closer to the courthouse as the faint sounds of the siren on the police jitney draws nearer. The roar rising from the crowd, interspersed with some choice cuss words from those being pushed back, is being ignored by the few policemen there, meant for keeping order amongst the crowd.

Ma Z sensing trouble ahead, through clenched teeth tosses to Josephine lying on the back seat, "don't play the fool today, stay in the car!" She knows that on hearing the siren, *Miss Josephine* would be inclined to rid herself of the flourbag over her and chance a peek out the car, maybe blowing her cover.

As the police jitney swings into the unpaved yard, its stop is sudden and jolting, its back wheels kicking up the clay-like dirt. To everyone's surprise, the always pedal pushing Mr. Brian is behind the steering wheel and is quickly rescued from an acutely embarrassing situation with this shout out; *"Man make up yuh mind, wah yuh really want to do, yuh have one foot on de brakes and de odder on the gas pedal!" "Lef de people vehicle alone and go back to yuh bike!"* Another admonishes. Yet a third chimes in, *"Lef de bike alone to Mr. Brian, plenty time I see yuh attempt to take a corner wide, wide and end up in a hibiscus fence or ditch." "Use a skater man, an' may God help yuh if yuh can't control dat too!"* Another hurls, as he doubles up with laughter of the preconceived visuals of Mr. Brian and the improvised wooden scooter ending up in the ditch at the side of some dirt truck.

Despite the picong and heckles that are being hurled, Mr. Brian remains resolute; he had received more abusive picongs in the past and he looks straight ahead as he gets out of the now properly parked vehicle.

Inside the still closed courthouse, reporters and cameramen for the major newspapers and radio stations, some professional sports personalities and even some local politicians are there, taking advantage of the cooling breezes from the ceiling fans. Mr. Brian is taking care of any prospective trouble, with the help of some past **'jailbirds'**, that he had befriended through the years. Those ex-convicts for whom he would often secure jobs, though never for themselves but for their mothers, sisters, girlfriends and wives, as servants for his prosperous business friends in the towns and far off city.

Those jobs with quick turnovers, Mr. Brian had access to, with madams and servants often getting into near fighting matches. Hence, the need for servants at the ready. To his ex and repeat jailbird friends, he would often turn a blind eye to their gambling or being runners for the illegal game of **'whe whe'**, as long as they troubled no one.

Mr. Brain spares nary a thought for One Man and his wanna be ***Bad Johns'***, his bully friends, the *'lightweights'*. He smiles as he steals a look at the scowling faces of Scarface, Bandito, Jingtoe, and Baby Face, jailbirds all. Small time convicts, each wearing his previous convictions as a badge of honor. Then, he turns and looks sneeringly into the eyes of *One Man et al*, their bottle and stones suddenly de-weaponized at the appearance of the ***'Real Bad Johns'***.

The crowd erupts in a deafening roar as Mr. Brian opens the back door of the van and out steps their hero, Joseph Celestine, cuffless but with one policeman ahead of him and another behind. He has emerged from his cage and is about to enter into the lion's den, into the Colosseum, the courthouse. Hopefully he's going in to slay the dragon, the lion, *et al*, to be victorious over whatever adversary that comes his way.

He smiles wanly, unsure of what all this means but is still ten foot tall to his people. He stops abruptly, his name is being shouted out. No one else has heard the pain in the voice that's calling out his name. His previously wan smile has disappeared and is replaced by one of longing and relief on clearly hearing her voice – but why hadn't she come to visit him?

The crowd eventually hearing her plaintive cries too, has made a path for her to get to him. As she approaches, she is unsure of what she should do, she keeps looking at the policemen who are gathered loosely around him. The policemen would not stop them from meeting and greeting each other. The village hero and would be heroine would have been married – he already achieved his status by competing locally and abroad and '*licking up*' the competition and she, meant to leave the village for the USA to sing and make records.

The policemen are relaxed; these two, they were after all and still *is* village people. They are all in this together, regardless on whose side they choose. There is this deafening silence from the crowd; not even a tweet coming from the usually chirping birds in the trees up above.

The crowd erupts in magnanimous applause as Joseph darts away from the understanding policemen and scoops up his love in his arms. He lifts her high in the air; they both are laughing and crying with happiness. Slowly, slowly, very slowly, he lowers her back to the ground now he takes her in his arms crushing her against him.

Abruptly he shoves her away at arms length, pain and disbelief registering in his widening eyes, as he looks down at her slightly swollen belly. He backs away from her shaking his head in utter disbelief. There are no words coming from Josephine – her hands now protectively over her swollen belly. Her eyes pleading for understanding. She loved him, they still love each other, always will!

Although she is following closely behind Josephine, Ma Z finds herself being pushed aside by the surging crowd with which she is fighting, she being just another faceless participant. She was afraid that something like this might happen and did not want to be a spectator, but Josephine was adamant in her demands to come to the courthouse, which she hesitantly gave into; not wanting Josephine's aggravation to have any adverse effect on her coming grandchild, her first. Maybe she should have listened to her friend Selma, let her win the fight and keep her precious taxi at home.

Ma Z finally gets through the unruly crowd, to the very front and is quickly enveloped as everyone else in the silence that prevails. She looks at the emotive changes in Joseph's face; the disbelief and utter contempt. He's holding her daughter at arms-length, evidently pushing her away, out of his life.

Josephine, with tear filled eyes, watches her Joseph walk away. She watches as he mounts the steps and into the courthouse to hear his fate. She keeps on rubbing her swollen stomach, hoping. She knows that she was reaching for the stars that are now clearly out of her reach, the perfect family. She knows that if her Joseph goes *away* no matter for whatever short a time, she would inevitably be blamed for his demise, yes, that's how it would seem. With hope for his continued successful career over and so too would the village hope of being prominently showcased on the cultural and sports map. Regretfully, inside the courthouse, their stars, hers and his were being dimmed, vanished!

Chapter 3

Ma Jo Jo is sweating beads of anxiety. She really, really does not want to entertain these thoughts. The past is the past the rotten regrettable past and then too, this storm, it's just mere hours away. She begins to think about the hen that she had roused from its comfortable bed in her carton below the house. Was the hen about to lay some eggs or to become a setting fowl? Wherever he is, Pa Joe Joe is having none of this; her being enraptured with her breezy thoughts in order to get away from their past. Ma Jo Jo begins to giggle like the schoolgirl she was, at the memory of their first meeting ...

Away in the distance, the schoolgirls heard the unmistakable shouts of the two horsemen cursing at them or maybe at their wild runaway horses. The horses seemingly wanting to get rid of the *beasts* on their backs, by bucking, standing on their hind legs and neighing horrendously.

Clearly the young village boys are at it again; pelting at the two men with green plums, guavas and young green mangoes. The young boys are motivated by the rumor making the rounds, which were most likely started by the young adults of the village, who are oftentimes clearly frustrated by the misbehavior of their young siblings, left in their charge, while their parents went off to work, in the nearby cocoa or coconut fields.

The rumor; that the two white horsemen, newcomers to the village and overseers to the Irish couple vast cocoa estate, were capturing the *bad children*, cutting them open to get their hearts and livers which they would feed to the horses, which enabled them to perform better, when eating only these organs of *bad* children.

This tale was fueled by the sudden disappearance of a *fresh up, womanish*, a very precocious young girl who in truth and in fact were secreted out of the village to other relatives, in order to end her involvement in an incestuous relationship.

As the still uncontrollable horses drew nearer, the children playing bat and ball in the middle of the dirt track, screamed to the high heavens and threw themselves into the drain at the side of the track.

Joseph Celestine and his friends, on hearing the terrified screams of Josephine and her friends, found them more petrified of the tadpoles and canal fishes crawling all over their bodies, than the supposedly murderous white men on the horses.

The 15-year-old Joseph and his friends plucked the much younger girls out of the canal. He holding onto the trembling Josephine's hands, letting her know that with him she'll always be safe.

~~~

Ma Jo Jo gets up from the upright cane chair and again tries to pick up from where she had left off, but her movements are lackluster and wooden. She's feeling frustrated with herself for not being able to reign in her thoughts about the past and '*him*' especially on a day like this one.

Again, Ma Jo Jo begins to gesticulate furiously whilst prancing around, her movements reeking of her frustrated feelings. She gives up; she must not fool herself. Her triumphs, happiness and gaiety in the past were too short lived, so definitely is no cause for celebrating anything now.

She had long willed away and succeeded in blanketing out the early years; the short loving magical years that she and Joseph Celestine shared. Their dreams for the future, while strolling hand in hand through the many lovers' lanes of this and other surrounding villages. Their sneaking off to the streams and pools; the pools which she particularly liked for the control movements of their waters, unlike the rivers. Lying wordlessly under the stars, on
~~~

beds of cool green grass wrapped in each other's arms, words between them need not be wasted. The respect they garnered from their peers. The envy from her friends; She having snagged the athlete, the hero who was sure to go places far and wide and he, the envy from his friends because he had snagged the village's golden voice.

Ma Jo Jo sighs and begins to sing in a sultry deep – throated voice. That Sarah Vaughn song, she would always sing in this tone and is surprised that after all these songless years she can still pull it off. Ma Jo Jo sighs again and it's full of nostalgia, she's remembering the first time that she had sang and earned a trophy. She had handed to Joseph the trophy that she had won *for him*. Telling him her victory was his too and he did likewise on winning a trophy or medal for his athletic prowess.

Tears are in Ma Jo Jo's eyes she is back to being the now 14-year-old who for the first time is walking hand in hand with the young man, the 17-year-old gazelle of the track and field fame. They are destined to be together; He is guiding her along the narrow tracks to the river, his strong lean fingers resting assuredly on the small of her back, then quickly to her shoulders on sensing her discomfort. He only wanting to steady her footsteps over the large stones and the sometimes-unsure terrain.

Ma Jo Jo smiles blissfully, that was the nature of her Joseph in whom she had complete trust, affording her the confidence to lose herself in the unspoilt and beautiful surroundings. Now, Ma Jo Jo is consumed with conflicting emotions of Pa Joe Joe. She can't stop herself from stepping back into their past, especially the regrettable parts that's now unreeling before her like a bad movie ...

There they are, standing under the coconut tree. He deftly shaving off the top off the water nuts with his long gleaming cutlass, as she waits patiently with the enamel mug in hand, into which he would pour the water of the shaven coconut. Now here it is about to climb onto his pants leg, the tarantula! Ma Jo Jo screams out in terror and in the process drops the just filled mug. Wide – eyed she looks up at him trembling and afraid; She feels a keen sense of confusion not knowing where the fear is coming from. She having encountered the spiders all her life. Is it him that she is perhaps afraid of; The love of her life, now, how could that be?

He in turn is looking down into her confused and terrified eyes. Is that what his years away have done to them? Pa Joe Joe feels a surge of compassion flooding his entire body, washing away the hate and anger that has been lodged in his heart, consuming him for all these years. He feels a satisfying warm glow spreading across his chest, to his now joyful fluttering heart. He can feel the sensation of the cracking an pulling apart of the artificial ice around his heart. He hears the roar of the walls of ice as it begins to crumble and melt.

Pa Joe Joe drops the cutlass that now seems to be burning his hand. He does not have to draw her into his arms, she is there even before the cutlass has hit the ground. He is encircling her with those two most powerful arms, crushing her against him.

He, being a few heads above her, she can feel and hear his wildly thumping heart, she can barely breathe but it is worth it. She dare not spoil this totally beautiful unexpected moment, this crazy exhilarating one! Gosh, how much it is worth it! She had wasted all those years, since his return...Ma Jo Jo's thoughts trail off.

Pa Joe Joe is smothering her with wild hungry kisses. Now, he pauses suddenly, gently pushing her away while looking deep into her eyes. He smiles and whispers all the silly things he used to tell her. Hoping that she can still laugh out loud as she often did, startling him back then. The promises, the plans that he would reveal for their future that would take her to the peaceful and secure place, causing her to snuggle even deeper into his encircling arms. He is hoping that she could feel that way once again.

Pa Joe Joe begins to croon their favorite Sarah Vaughn song; the one that she had taught him ...oh yes he could sing too! He lifts her high, high, higher and higher – way up there, as if wanting her to touch the branches of the coconut tree. Something he would have done unsteadily before, though never letting her fall. This time his trusting her way up there is sure. Five years of pumping iron and lifting weights would see to that, his strength, his arms. He keeps on looking deep into her eyes, seeing the hurt and pain that he has caused her. Her giddy, free laughter isn't there anymore.

Suddenly a cold and steely feeling envelops him. If he was doing this to her, causing her this immeasurable pain, he wasn't sure how he could stop now; wasn't even sure that he wanted to anyway, after all, it was she who had destroyed what could have been.

For the five years he was away from her, Pa Joe Joe would from time to time relive the courthouse scene, torturing himself on discovering *her betrayal*, he held onto that thought in order to make sense of the hell, the madness that had descended on so many people through his actions.

On becoming a Preacher Man, he helped the many around him to save their souls, but Pa Joe Joe could not save his. Her torturous cries for help; he finding her lying there on the beautiful green grass, his blade coming down again and again; The blood leaping up staining the heavens then coming angrily down, soiling the pure green grass; Her betrayal destroyed his soul!

Still up in the air in Pa Joe Joe's steady hands, Ma Jo Jo is looking through the tall trees and cluster of bushes. She is looking at the fading sun slinking away. She is feeling the pressure of Pa Joe Joe's strong fingers as they clench her waist, causing a bit of discomfort to which she does not complain. For these magical moments she would endure even more.

His fingers are tightening around her waist like a vise, holding on for dear life, begging her to save them from him. Ma Jo Jo is helpless since she too is beginning her own fight. She is hearing the squeaking hinges of the top half of the wooden kitchen door, as it is being opened. Ma Jo Jo sees the tiny fingers holding onto the still latched bottom half of the door. She doesn't see her but pretty soon she expects to see the top of the fibrous uncombed hair of the small child. She, now up from her forced afternoon nap, would be steadying her sea legs and will be on tippy toes peering over the door.

The child had scampered up from her makeshift bed off crocus bags, topped with flour sacks and an old sheet in a corner of the living room floor and on determining that she was alone in the house, began her search for Ma Jo Jo, hoping that she had not run off and left her – her constant fear.

Now on tippy toes, her eyes barely above the door, the child has ascertained that her unfounded fear could be put to rest for another episode of waking up from one of her forced afternoon naps. Sure enough, Ma Jo Jo is looking back into two deep black pools of nothingness on the child's blank face - the face that often puzzles as well as frightens her.

The *Older One*, the nickname given and stuck to her by many of the neighborhood women, who thought of her as being *womanish*, one who was *here before*, too beyond her years, a precocious child. Ma Jo Jo didn't like the labels but there were times because of the child's behavior, she silently agreed.

Ma Jo Jo hears the '*click, clack*' as the Older One unlatches the door and slowly descends the few steps. Her thumb and one corner of her blanket stuck in her mouth – the blanket still in a tight hold because she is not fully awake. Ma Jo Jo is willing her to get back, back into the house – back to whatever dream she had awoken from, to just stay away! Ma Jo Jo herself does not want to be awaken, does not want the wonderful dream in which she is now enraptured to be over.

Ma Jo Jo is silently begging her, the Older One, to please not spoil what could be a momentous outcome – she and Joseph Celestine finding their way back to each other. Yes, even if it was only in a dream.

Pa Joe Joe's deep melodious voice cuts through Ma Jo Jo's thoughts. She quickly shifts her eyes and attention away from the two dark bottomless pools on the child's face and focuses on her tall strong Adonis who still has her way above in the air. What a voice he possesses, she muses. She sees the tears nestled in the corner of his eyes. The pain, the despair but most of all the disguised frustration or anger perhaps?

She gently removes her hand from his shoulders and solidifies her position by wrapping her legs around the strong and still slender torso. She need not have fear, because he would not let her fall, no never!

Ma Jo Jo begins to trace the outline of his face as she joins him in the rendition of their Sarah Vaughn song. Mo Jo Jo's voice has now devolved into a whisper, as she searches through the branches of the far-off trees that's blocking out the view of anything beyond them. She scans the heavens and sees that the low riding clouds are being tossed about like beach balls by the actions of the strong mischievous winds.

With a sense of sadness, she finally glimpses the sun as it slips away leaving a black void where it sat and is no longer weaving its way through the trees and bushes, kissing everything in its path.

Through the coconut tree branches, she is looking at a tangle of barren fruit trees at the swamp. The bottlenecked avocado, mangoes, and breadfruit trees, canceling out each other for the sunlight and breathing spaces. Yes, choking each other from ever being fruitful. She shakes her head angrily at the black cloud hovering over them.

On the ground the little black cloud with the blanket is tumbling, rolling, galloping and now stomping towards them. Ma Jo Jo quickly slips her hands over Pa Joe Joe's ears, she does not want him to hear the feet of the marching army, the soldiers coming to conquer them, this time not just for five years but to vanquish them, ground them to dust! The end is upon them. Ma Jo Jo cannot or maybe just does not want to will away the little black cloud anymore; Her hands fall away from Pa Joe Joe's ears.

Giggling nervously and with her blanket trailing behind her, the Older One reaches up and timidly touches Pa Joe Joe's back. Ma Jo Jo's heart melts, she looks down at the too often sucked wrinkled thumb of the Older One. With her both arms outstretched, hoping that Pa Joe Joe would turn around and scoop her up, lifting her high up into the heavens, as he is doing to Ma Jo Jo. Yes, she is reaching out to the unseeing Pa Joe Joe.

Puzzled at the touch, Pa Joe Joe trails off from rendering his version of yet another Sarah Vaughn song he has just started. He quickly puts Ma Jo Jo down; pained, he looks at the outstretched arms and makes as if he's going to ignore her but then he bends and rumples the uncombed hair. His hands lying hesitantly on her head – his eyes unreadable, his jaws twitching uncontrollably. He looks across at Ma Jo Jo and says dully, "You didn't leave me then as I asked you too; this time you've got to do it, leave me now!"

Ma Jo Jo can hear the steel door of his heart slamming shut. She wonders, was that how the steel doors of the jail being shut, must have sounded behind him? With such finality, to the young and frightened Joseph Celestine? Once more he was shutting her out of his life, for good this time, leaving her devoid of every emotion, leaving her empty, a woman of straw.

Chapter 4

Ma Jo Jo makes an attempt to go back to her cane bottomed chair but on hearing the sudden crack and eventual fall of what seems to be a large limb of one of the fruit trees, that she creeps across the room to peer through a crack of one of her wooden windows.

She sees the bench on which she was sitting just a few hours ago. From that perch she did glance up at the ominous looking cloud that appeared and somehow stayed hovering over her humble home. She was not afraid of it – it was welcome to stay and do its dance of death. She smiles wondering if Pa Joe Joe was the one in there doing the dance – she shrugs her shoulders in a *don't care damn way*. If he is still bent on punishing her, there's nothing she could do about it. If he is in complete control of things now, she only hopes that he would not make the whole village pay for her sins.

Ma Jo Jo cannot help herself, she dissolves in tears and looks upward. She's thinking about the time Pa Joe Joe looked at her and cried out dispassionately that she was dead, dead inside. Ma Jo Jo was flabbergasted, she did not know where this was coming from, his cry of utter contempt, of scorn.

He did not mean what he had just said to her, couldn't! He had loved her from the start, loved his Josephine just as she loved him. Her loving kind Joseph Celestine was in there somewhere, she had to believe that! Again, Ma Jo Jo reaches back, this time only two weeks ago ...

~~~
~~~

...Pa Joe Joe's death; His wake, the singers, the pulsating drums, the wild frenzied footwork of the dancers. Her hiding behind the black drapes in her bedroom trying to replicate the moves of the dancers. Her singing along to the must sung, song of wake nights. The name of the composer she never knew; *'tonight is the bongo night'* ... Ma Jo Jo trails off. She doesn't wish to participate anymore in this wake business, this prelude to his burial.

Suddenly, she is in deep turmoil, she is reaching even further back to more troubling times too. She's bringing forth the young Josephine, her final performance for the villagers before she goes abroad. She is supposed to be rendering her favorite Sarah Vaughn and Anita Baker hits. She's in the middle of the stage; the *'combo'* is playing low, low, in the background. The crowd is excited and vociferous. Now, she is running away from her adoring fans, running through those high weeds and tall bushes. She falls, Mr. Leo is coming towards her! The grass she is lying on surely does not feel or smell like the soft carpet of green grass that she and the young Joseph Celestine would lie on, gazing up at the sky and the all-knowing twinkling stars and smiling '**Mr. Moon**'.

The knife is coming down over and over with the blood spurting upwards as if coming from an uncapped geyser and falling back down in ugly clumps. Soiling, ruining the previously pristine grass and staining their future.

~~~

Ma Jo Jo screams out as if in unstoppable severe pain and is transported back from her regrettable past into her equally regrettable present. She looks around and sighs guiltily. For days the news on the radio were all about the coming storm. Even two *official* looking men had been dispatched in a car with *'loudspeakers'* atop, to traverse the village, to every nook and cranny where the vehicle could safely drive, broadcasting the news of the coming storm. These broadcasts at every lull, were replaced by calypso music, blasting through the loudspeakers.

Ma Jo Jo was thoroughly fed up with the storm '**dis**', storm '**dat**', everything storm, storm, storm! She wishes for more reason
~~~

than one, that when it comes, that it would take her away just as it would be taking away large sections of the village; if the news coming from the local grapevine were to be believed. That it would bury her deep in the pools of mud where the cattle would be trapped. Surely wherever her is, Pa Joe Joe probably thinks that's where she belongs too – The swamp her burial place.

Again, her thoughts go back to earlier in the day, with her seated on the bench under the *zaboca* tree. Within a matter of seconds on hearing the rustling of the tree, a laden branch with bottlenecked avocados came crashing down. She sat there, contemplating how on earth, after gathering all those avocados, would she be able to take them inside the house. She looked questioningly at the rickety steps thinking about her unsteadily climbing them with dozens of the fruit in her arms.

With a puzzled look on her face she wondered, is Pa Joe Joe trying to tell her something through those increasingly unsteady steps beneath her feet? Ma Jo Jo sighed and shook her head. This annoying pastime had become her looking for signs that Pa Joe Joe was communicating with her but in essence, she was driving herself crazy!

Now, she shakes her shoulders with indifference. Everything around her has suddenly begun to crumble; she begins to think about the rain now pouring through a rotting galvanized sheeting covering the gallery. She sighs yet again, Pa Joe Joe would have known how to fix this, fix many things, her Pa Joe Joe did.

She smiles at her perceived visuals of him, of his bulging muscles under the '*holey*' merino, this, his work one drenched in sweat, his musclebound forearms likened to two small hams, she chuckled at the thought. The droplets of sweat dispensing, falling off like rain drops as he'd swing his axe chopping away at the logs needed for firewood to feed the clay oven outback, as she prepared the dough for the coconut bakes, pones and sweet breads that soon would be baked – regular weekend chores, undertaken by most households in the village.

Ma Jo Jo musings comes to an abrupt end as she shakes her head vigorously as if to empty it of all her useless thoughts at a time like this. She *cheupses* slowly and turns around quickly, surprised that she has sucked her teeth this long and loudly. Then, ashamedly smacks herself upside her head, although there is no one around to hear her or see her antics.

~~~

Ma Jo Jo got up from the bench and began to pluck the avocados from off the fallen branch. She first thought about placing them in her skirt but then realized that they were much too much to be placed in her very flared skirt even though it was supported at the waist by the biggest of *safety pins*.

She looked around again for something else in which to store them, her avocados. She saw the wheelbarrow but it was filled with weeds and twigs, that two days ago she had pulled from her kitchen garden near the pens of her pet pigs, Willy, Daisy and Mr. Brown but had neglected to dump on her compost pile because of the riotous behavior of those three.

Ma Jo Jo just could not deal with their behavior at that time of day. They, who on seeing or even *'smelling'* her would break out in very riotous behavior, they, always expecting her to be bringing them swill. Ma Jo Jo smiles at the remembrance of Pa Joe Joe laughingly pointing out their effusive greetings as she made her way to them. Momentarily, Ma Jo Jo thoughts grows dark, very dark. Did he mean that it was only her pigs who were happy to see her?

Ma Jo Jo shook her head again and looked around for something large enough to store the avocados. She espied a cardboard box under the house. Getting it posed a problem – this box which she was lucky enough to extract from the Chineseman shopkeeper without a cost, he selling everything. Previously filled flour and crocus bags, empty *'pitch oil'* and cooking oil tins, literally anything! For the past few days those always in need of items, had become hot commodities because of the coming storm; The tins needed to store extra water and the bags for emergency bedding.

The box under the house now housed a setting hen who definitely would not want to give it up, *'her maternity ward'*, her nest. But then Ma Jo Jo knew that the hen had not too long claimed the box because she had seen her in the fowl run, scratching at the earth
~~~

and pecking away at the small insects that she had unearthed. Ma Jo Jo determined that if she could get the box away from the hen, she would fill it with the avocados and easily climbed the stairs with the filled box, empty its contents on her kitchen table, then bring it back to the hen who could have it for eternity.

Ma Jo Jo hesitated a bit after looking at the hen who seemed to be very comfortable. Then with a steely resolve, determined that the box was hers and not the hens – *'too besides'* the hen had her place. The fowl run was equipped with coops and bedding, straw, suited for the purpose of this hen and there she should really be!

Ma Jo Jo looked around for something to protect herself from the hen who seemed ready and capable to engage her in a battle for the box, which by right was hers! She settled for a broom which she herself had made. The broomstick cut from a long lean and sturdy branch from one of the guava trees at the back of the pig pens and the thistles from an assortment of flexible bushes that she had cut from the side of the track leading to the river. These she placed at one end of her broomstick and tied together from a strip of a bed sheet no longer in use.

With trepidation, some grains in one hand and the broom which she hoped would not be used in the other, Ma Jo Jo approached her unwanted tenant in the cardboard box, clucking all the way. Ma Jo Jo bent low, eyeballing the hen, the hen did the same thing, eyeballed her.

Ma Jo Jo began her cluck, cluck, clucking sounds once more, as she tossed her grains of corn away from the disinterested hen who did not take kindly with her, Ma Jo Jo trying to *'mamaguy'* her, fool her with a few grains of corn, she being smarter *'dan dat'*! No, she did not fall for Ma Jo Jo trying to butter her up when her intention was really to get her out of the carton.

The hen did get up but not out of the box – she, clucking loudly and angrily, swiveling her neck and flapping her wings – she was also scratching furiously in the box. This hen was clearly disturbed, ready for a fight maybe?

Ma Jo Jo who seems able to communicate with every animal and bird in her yard, no matter how unintelligible the sound, leaving her neighbors snickering behind her back, just could not get through to Lucille the hen.

It was a common sight to see the chickens and fowls following Ma Jo Jo down the hill every other Thursday morning when she would leave the village for the city to do the heavy shopping for her animals; to buy the bulk goods and on completion, hire a taxi to bring her back to the village.

On reaching the bottom of the hill, while waiting on the bus Ma Jo Jo would turn around and shoo the birds back up the hill, looking on as every last one obediently and in single file fled up the hill, disappearing to the back of the house in the unfenced yard.

Ma Jo Jo sensing that there would be no cooperation from Lucille the mother hen, poked the box a few times with the broom. By her head movements and indiscernible noises Lucille seemed mightily ruffled an offended. Frustrated, Ma Jo Jo straightened up, gently rubbing her neck, trying to get rid of the painful kink she had developed by being in the awkward stooping position. Her knees too, seemed relieved to be released from being bent and under the strain of her weight.

The sudden thunderclap as it rolled across the heavens startled Ma Jo Jo. It seemed to have done the same to Lucille, who immediately picked up where she had left off with her clucking and frenetic movements. Ma Jo Jo turned around, scanning what she could see of the sky through the intertwining branches of all the different variety of fruit trees. They absolutely obstructing the sun and what other elements from filtering through. Startled once again as another peal of thunder followed by a display of near blinding lightning got to her below the house, Ma Jo Jo *jumped out of her skin* then quickly steeled herself. The bushbroom in her hand, unintentionally becoming weaponized as she went after her beloved Lucille with the battering ram, poking at the box with brute force. The box toppled over and but for a moment, she was awashed in shame and sorrow.

Relieved that there were no eggs in the box to be broken, Ma Jo Jo knew that she had just a few moments to get away from the angry bird who had once again begun her clucking and furiously scratching at the ground. Her wings expanded wide as if ready to launch an attack against Ma Jo Jo too.

Ma Jo Jo beat a hasty retreat dropping and leaving the bushbroom in her wake as she scurried inside the wooden shed and shut the door behind her. She heard the hen who had followed, furiously pecking at the door of the makeshift shed. She knew that if the bird was not so stupid, it could have gotten inside – the walls of the unfinished shed, not reaching up to the roof. She had often seen *this* miss Lucille and other fowls in the yard, even those unclipped ducks and one lone turkey roosting there most nights.

Ma Jo Jo on tippy toes, peeped over one side of the shed – she took in the broom that she had dropped in her wake, the unplucked zabocas still attached to the fallen branch and the wheelbarrow sitting idle as if waiting for someone to come and rid it of the pulled and wilted weeds sitting inside.

She smiled at the sight of the hen sitting once again, unbothered in her somewhat toppled over box. Ma Jo Jo sighed, looking around the shed, her prison for the moment; A lot of good she had done herself in trying to establish ownership of the box.

Still on tippy toes Ma Jo Jo moved to another side of the shed and peeped over the wall which is quite shorter. She looked into her neighbor's yard, their shared unfenced yard. A tinge of jealousy clouds her eyes. Unlike hers, the immediacy of Ma Cedeno's yard is bereft of all those giant fruit trees. Ma Cedeno's were sensibly planted way out to the back, where they did not hinder the growth of her low lush vegetable garden, the constant object of Ma Jo Jo's envious eyes. Ma Jo Jo who seemed to think that the lush kitchen garden, it's vibrantly hued red, green and yellow vegetation, always seemed to be smiling mockingly at her.

Chapter 5

Ma Jo Jo's chest is heaving, her throat is so dry and parched that the songs coming forth are raspy and guttural. A good decision, she thinks of her abandoning the attempt to sing the song of Nancy Wilson, another singing sensation. She's listless, her radio has suddenly stopped playing – just some annoying gibberish sounds seem to be coming forth, no matter what knobs she fiddles with. She even replaced the batteries, fairly new ones, with unused ones – no luck! She attributes this to the storm which has really begun to pick up momentum.

She picks up the enamel cup of bush tea and takes few quick sips of the still warm liquid. This tea was piping hot when just made but like everything in Ma Jo Jo's life it was momentarily forgotten when she started her musings of Pa Joe Joe.

She moves from the bedroom to the drawing room, where she opens one of the board windows, just a crack. She squints at the looming figure approaching in the darkness; She squints again as the figure draws near. She sees that it's Elvin; she is surprised that she did not see the donkey behind him the very first time. She is also surprised that she didn't hear the loud coaxing and *'sweet talking'* to the donkey that he would usually have to do to get the animal out of or in its shed. This donkey that he has refused to put out to pasture, *to retire* as some of his friends would mockingly cajole him to do. **Both he and the donkey**, some would derisively suggest behind his back. To his face, some would *buss fatigue* of his owning the only donkey in the village that would only *skin teeth*, grin but not bray, the non – braying jackass, they would guffaw.

Elvin was tired of their attempt of humor at his and his donkey's expense. He would be *pelted* with those stale and tired jokes from his so-called friends as they *limed* under the Chineseman's shop. Yes, that's where they hung out, right in front of the shop every Saturday morning as he took the donkey to the river to have her bath. Sometimes he wished that there was an alternative route to the river where he would not have to see those deriding *Imps*, those mischievous friends but there they would surely be. Gambling for pennies while keeping a wary eye out for the bike riding policeman, Mr. Brian or any one of his foot patrolling compatriots who were tasked with the job of squelching the new plague of fowl thievery, even in broad daylight that descended on the village – a new phenomenon.

The villagers swore that the thief or thieves were outsiders, they being respectful of each other and would not commit such a vile and abominable sin as stealing from each other when all they had to do was ask and would receive. The young men might pelt at a tempting ripe mango or other fruit in a neighbor's yard or pull some root vegetable from a garden to boil in a pot as a *side*, to eat with the wild meat, that they had caught the night before in the forest and most assuredly would *'stew down'* in an iron pot down by the river. Stealing livestock, never, they would swear on their ancestor's graves!

The villagers knew that things were getting serious when old man Sheppy *'lost'* two roosters and his prized fighting cock, which he would enter in competitions far and wide. His cocks *'licking up'* the competition, winning every fight and gaining for old man Sheppy more notoriety in his old age than he had as a young man on the wharf in the city.

The grief stricken 89-year-old man with his walking stick in one hand and in the other, his *'gilpin'*, it's dangerous looking blade gleaming, would carré with his weapon in hand anytime he saw a group of young men. All suspicious looking to his eyes; his grieving eyes. His increasingly demented mind irrationally linking them with his lost birds. They in turn having to *'duck'*, make evasive movements whenever he brandished his gilpin, his dangerous looking cutlass near them; Even though deep down they knew that he would never lay it on them.

These young men of the village, having nothing to do with the disappearance of his or any of the other villager's birds, decided to band together to apprehend whoever was responsible. They began patrolling the tracks and traces *'foreday'* mornings, yes in the very early hours of the mornings, even lying in wait in the bushes and grasses behind the fowl coops, night after night or even crouched up in some of the coops themselves, with their sharpened *gilpins*, *pouyas* or whatever name were befitting their weapons at hand.

The planned *plannassing* of the culprit or culprits was a sure thing. Their proper *cutail* or sound beating was *booked* for the revolting and criminal act of robbing the elderly, since most of the losses were suffered by them.

Luckily for all, the concerned constable Mr. Brian, as he is wont to do, heard of the vigilante, planned actions by the youths and decided that he could have none of that so he put some of his *'Bad John'* friends' on the *case* to get any information back to him.

Not unexpectedly, an informed constable Brian in the early hours of one morning, came upon the two youngsters quickly trying to douse the fire under a boiling pot of root vegetables cooking, minus fowl of any kind. They had stopped taking the villagers fowls on hearing about the planned *'cutails'*.

On interrogation it was learned that the two youths were recent residents of the boy's industrial school in the nearby town and now officially non – residents, they did not wish to go back to the town from which day came. They begged to continue their *'residency'* in the cave like shelter near the waterfall.

With crestfallen faces, the two youth men stood before Ma Jo Jo, Mr. Sheppy, Mr. and Mrs. Cedeno, Elvin's parents and some of the skeptical young men who had valiantly laid in the dewy grasses and their cramped positions in the coops for the fowl thieves who never came.

On looking at the two shamefaced young men and learning of their troubling circumstance, Mr. Sheppy cleared his throat, quickly concluding that all was forgiven especially when he heard that his birds, especially the prized cock fighting Gabriel was not eaten but sold to a competitor, one village away and who by now was surely enjoying '*his*' birds, by engaging in cock fighting arenas in far off villages. Mr. Sheppy bristled at the thought that his competitor were in receipt of his prize birds, especially Gabriel which Mr. Brian swore to recover, if still alive. To this the two young men swore that they have seen the birds alive, when they visited the son of the *new owner*, their friend and fellow resident of the boy's industrial school.

Mr. Sheppy smiled whimsically as he recalled his own youth and his exploits with his friend Ralphie, not unlike these two youth men in front of him. Then he suddenly grew grim – why did he do it, go back dredging up the past? His blood began *to boil*, he began to grow angry as he recalled what *buss up* their friendship for the last time ...

It was customary of some of the workers on the wharf to gamble on any of *their breaks*, short or long. Ralphie the leader of the group of disparate gamblers, was in charge of the card games, including the '*pot*'. It was bad enough that Ralphie manipulated the card games, but he did not even share in some of his ill-gotten gains with Mr. Sheppy, whenever he slyly dug his hands into the pot.

The doggone scamp Mr. Sheppy fumed when finding out just how Ralphie did it! Wave after wave of nostalgia washed over him and Mr. Sheppy teared up on realizing that he was missing his friend and the good old days, even his scampishness too, plus the loads of trouble that he would get them in for his sometimes-childish pranks. After some quiet moments Mr. Sheppy smiled fondly thinking; *he did get us out of quite a few too*. He smiled again on coming to the conclusion that Ralphie, was not an entirely bad person, that there were really two Ralphie's in that one personage and began to count the good things that Ralphie did. Then after racking his brains in his deliberate search and not being able to come up with more than five good deeds in their years together, Mr. Sheppy gave up.

Mr. Sheppy shrugged his shoulders wishing his long dead and gone friend good luck in trying to rob the devil and his imps in their card games and more so in trying to cheat the *cheat* himself out of his cut in any ill-gotten gains.

Mr. Sheppy knew that he was being spiteful and frustratingly so, in his wishes for his friend Ralphie because of his faulty memory glitches. Five good deeds indeed! Ralphie did boat loads of good deeds Mr. Sheppy quickly conceded and promised to say the whole rosary for Ralphie before going to bed. He then chuckled at the thought of Ralphie seeing him praying, yes he, the convict.

~~~

Now, on hearing that Mr. Brian had caught the fowl thieves, a larger group of villagers quickly encircled the two bewildered looking young boys. They, the agitated villagers, had grabbed onto broomsticks, pots and pans and even twigs that they pulled from the bushes on their way, to give to them, the finest *cutail* of their lives, only to encounter these pitiful looking souls.

Mr. Sheppy was doing a lot of grunting, humming and hawing while deep in thought as he scratched his head and gnawed on his empty pipe. Eventually he motioned for Mr. Brian whom he regarded as the son he never had, to come over to him. He then implored the policeman to give the youths another chance to straighten out their lives and that he would take it upon himself to guide them.

Seeing the hesitancy in Mr. Brian's eyes, Mr. Sheppy decided to take a gamble, albeit a painful one – heck, these boys lives, or futures were on the line. He steeled himself and let the cold harsh words tumble out of his mouth, "remember Chance your brother; Chance, do this in memory of him."

Mr. Sheppy looked at Mr. Brian's face and saw every drop of blood leave that tortured face. Mr. Brian turned and walked away, both hands held up in the air in total surrender. He only stopped to take the bicycle that he had left propped up against the hibiscus fence. Mr. Sheppy kept looking after Mr. Brian, who kept on walking at the side of the bicycle; suddenly too weak to mount it. Then, he slumped down at the side of the track bringing the bike to rest beside him.

Mr. Sheppy sighed deeply; he did not mean to hurt Mr. Brian, did not want the torturous memory of his brother to flood him, but he did what he had to do. He had just saved two young men from going the way of Chance. Soon, they would learn to fish and hunt with the young men of the village, learn to till the land too and Mr. Brain would appreciate this in time to come.
~~~

Mr. Sheppy smiled on seeing a beautiful red, green and gold feather, glittering above in the stillness of the evening – it was doing a little dance for him in the windless sky; soaring way above the houses of Miss Carmen and Ma Jo Jo, swooning, dipping and twirling above the houses. He smiled again, it was her, wasn't it?

Mr. Sheppy became embarrassed by the tears brimming his eyes and moved to the far side of the yard, away from the neighbors still milling about the yard, even after the departure of Mr. Brian. Some had seen the tears before he moved away and had smiles on their faces – they understood the tears and his gaze skyward. Then they eventually began to file out of the yard. Miss Cedeno did too, taking the two young men with her, they needed to be fed.

Miss Cedeno instinctively knew that Mr. Sheppy would be housing the two young men in his tool shed. After they were fed, she would have Elvin and his friends clear and clean the shed. She began to muse about the coming darkness – she needn't have worried. The boys of the village were very handy with flambeaus, big and small. She looked across at the shed: they, some of the neighborhood women would spruce it up after its cleaning. The two young men belonged to them now, the neighborhood.

They left Mr. Sheppy gazing up into the sky – into her still beautiful face; The face that would never grow old. "Now, go away my sweet little one, go rest", he whispered to the feather, that as if by magic, fluttered down and tickled his nose.

The feather did not immediately soar up and away but kept on gliding and twirling above his head, doing its little dance – she loved to dance too. "Go away," he again softly coaxed the feather. The feather still stayed above his head. With tears freely rushing down his cheeks, Mr. Sheppy tried again, his lips quivering now; "I promise, promise to join you shortly," then he gently blew on the feather.

Through his bleary eyes Mr. Sheppy watched as the feather finally took flight, somehow managing to soar into the windless sky, until it disappeared into the silverest of clouds. Then he labored up the short flight of steps and closed the door behind him. Quickly, he opened it again as if hoping to catch a glimpse of the long-gone feather. Instead, his eyes beheld the rainbow, a strange phenomenon at this time of evening, its colors the most vivid he ever did see. "Yes! Yes! Yes!" He shouted with confidence sure that the feather and the rainbow were apparitions of his wife Miss Nan. With a sense of finality, he closed the door and stumbled to the bed on which he involuntarily collapsed...

Chapter 6

Ma Jo Jo stomps her feet; They are uncomfortably cramped – she is not aware that she had been standing motionless for such a long time. She is standing with her forehead pressed against the board window in her bedroom. She, peering at Elvin trying to coax his donkey to walk the few more yards to its stall in the back of his house, but the donkey just would not move, not one foot!

Probably trying to outsmart his donkey into thinking that he did not care to go anywhere, Elvin folded his arms and stood at the side of his animal, the rain pouring down on them. Trying to test the adage, **stubborn as a mule**, perhaps?

Ma Jo Jo was about to decide which of them is really the ass, when Elvin's best friend Roland, rides up on his bicycle and after a quick discussion, gets off the bike and behind the animal, tries pushing it. The animal responds with a few flick of its tail, some catching Roland on his face.

Ma Jo Jo anticipates the argument that is about to ensue between the clearly annoyed Roland and Elvin who is doubling up with laughter and stomping his feet in the muddy water.

Ma Jo Jo is looking at his antics with alarm. Doesn't he know that his shoes are *'laughing'*, the both fronts are unstuck, and his toes are peeping out; That he is apt to get *ground itch*, with his feet exposed in the dirty water?

Ma Jo Jo keeps looking at the stupid young man and wondering if he had caught some sort of *'laughing fits'*. He tosses back his head *'kyah kayhing'*, then holding onto his belly and going low, low down to the ground, weak with laughter, the seat of his pants touching the wet ground.

Suddenly, Ma Jo Jo's ears perk – up, did she just hear a Hee – Haw, coming from the donkey? Its first ever Hee Haw, if she harkens back to the claims of Elvin's picong giving friends.

She presses her forehead further into the board window as if that's possible; Squinting and blinking her watery eyes. Sure, enough she has heard correctly. The two friends no longer going at each other, has heard it too and are now standing in front of the donkey, trancelike. Hee haw! Hee haw! Hee haw! The donkey adds another *hee haw* for emphasis.

The two friends are laughing and prancing around in the muddy trace with glee. Elvin's toes are coming clear out of the front of his laughing shoes, the busted shoes now useless on his feet.

Ma Jo Jo looks at the incredible scene unfolding; she blinks as the friend moves behind the donkey on his mounted bike and with his hand now on the donkey's back and Elvin with the end of rope from around its neck, they manage to get the previously obstinate animal to the shed behind the house.

Ma Jo Jo stays at the window stomping her numb feet until she sees the last of Elvin, the donkey and Roland on his bike, his hands now on the donkey's rump. Elvin, the young man, he reminds her so much of her Joseph – young kind and *so much in love with her*, she adds hastily.

With that, Ma Jo Jo yet again slips back into her yesterdays... Joseph on his trusty old bicycle making a run to the market or dry goods shop for Ma Baker, just as he would for Miss Jean. He, with the empty plastic buckets on the handles of his bike; The friends he had managed to encourage to do likewise, following behind. Even those with the empty vessels in their box carts trotting behind in their search for water for some of the dependent elderly. The dry season also meant that there would be no water flowing from the hissing standpipes at the side of the traces.

That's when Joseph Celestine and his friends always stepped in, going from stream to stream, once dependable watering holes now dried up and they the young men at the mercy of the unforgiving blistering sun.

To the young men these jaunts in search of water, were more like outings; Gladly undertaken, taking them away from fretful mothers or big sisters not satisfied with the hastily swept yards or amount of firewood, chopped for the coalpots that were to be used outside.

~~~

Ma Jo Jo sighs and moves away from the board window. Then with a series of listless twirls is in her drawing room once again. She pulls at the highly polished mahogany rocking chair at the equally highly polished center table. She looks amusingly at the Christmas and Easter cards, some as far back as three years ago, lying on the doilie decorating the small round table.

She only now realizes that the chair she is tugging at, has become resistant because it's stuck on the thick shaggy rug on which it sits. The crocus bag rug on which she had artfully and skillfully designed and woven a basket of flowers from small strips of colorful cotton, with the help of two hair clips. She was very proud of the oohs! and ahhs! Coming from the neighbors who came to view her end product.

Even the Irish woman from up the hill near the waterfall, came and was completely blown away by Ma Jo Jo's artistry and ended up ordering three such rugs. Yes, the same patterns, even though Ma Jo Jo had boastfully assured her that she was capable of weaving even better patterns. Truthfully, Ma Jo Jo was dreading the drudgery of having to work on the same patterns and becoming bored in the process.

Of the three rugs that the Irish woman ordered, one would be for herself, one for her beloved mother and reluctantly, the other for her older sister with whom she had been feuding, after having been appraised by a visiting relative of the mother's declining health since she, the younger daughter left Ireland for these shores. The older daughter was not **'dropping'** in on the mother enough but
~~~

just depending on the help that she had gotten for her through some distant relative.

Having completed the task of coaxing and dragging the previously stuck chair from the rug, Ma Jo Jo plops down, her head resting way back and deep down into the cushion, her plump hands on its arms. She begins to rock furiously and decides to sing her favorite Sarah Vaughn song but instead of that gentle soothing song gliding out of her mouth, a raucous and coarse calypso comes tumbling out. Ma Jo Jo ends the song and immediately straightens up. Did this happen, the coarse song, because of her furious rocking? She is puzzled and blushes at her choice of song. With Pa Joe Joe gone she seems to be indulging in things that would not have met with his approval – she blushes again.

Her eyes welling up, they travel down her gaily flowered skirt, to her customary bare feet and beholds the dead bird lying there. Was that the reason why she was getting so much trouble in moving the chair? Is this '*him*' trying to tell her something? Does he want her to just sit here and look at what she has done to him? Killed his dreams, then his spirit, though so many years ago?

Utterly frustrated, the very restless Ma Jo Jo gets up and walks away. She keeps looking back at the chair that seems to be still rocking by unseen hands. The very superstitious Ma Jo Jo for the umpteenth time, promises that this time, to finally rid herself of the chair, by giving it to the young men who at their next cookout on the hill, would feed it to the fires under one of their large filled iron pots. The fires would hopefully consume the bad spirits that live within it. *'That's the way he wants it, that's the way he's going to get it'*. Ma Jo Jo somehow surmises at the presence of the dead bird and the resistant rocking chair.

She moves to the kitchen where she takes the large enamel cup, her special '*dipper*', to her newest water container, a five-gallon previous cooking oil container, which she had bought from the Chineseman's shop. Scrubbing it out before filling it with the spring water. The same containers filled with water that Elvin and his friends would deliver as per their custom to the elderly or those with no one to help them in their homes. Ma Jo Jo giggles because she knows that she does not fit the above bill, only that she is just, the wife of their dearly departed Pa Joe Joe.

Sipping at the water drawn from the previous oiltin, Ma Jo Jo begins to worry about the price she paid for the tin; $1.50, a drastic increase of 75 cents! She begins to think about this spiraling cost of living in everything now. Were these charges caused by the city and towns people sudden encroachment amongst the *'**country boukies**'*, the villagers?

She now begins to weigh the pluses or minuses of her having a cup of bush tea or one of cocoa. Eventually the bush tea wins out as she recalls having seen only two pack of cocoa powder in her '*safe*'; The cabinet where she keeps all her '*messages*', her groceries.

Ma Jo Jo steups loudly, she is decidedly frustrated by the thought of the coming storm and what it is putting the villagers through. Why doesn't it stop '*coming*' and come? She wonders highly annoyed.

Suddenly her eyes widen as she '*cocks*' her head and again wonders, 'Is it already here?' She listens to the rain pounding on the galvanized roof and the winds furiously blowing and snapping off the branches from the trees around her house. As she's been doing all along, Ma Jo Jo steups again, and begins fiddling once more with the knobs of her radio and miraculously gets it centered enough so she can hear the voice of the broadcaster, painting a decidedly worrisome and ominous picture that surely hints at the devastation, maybe obliteration too, of some villages in the far off eastern portion of the island – those *that's really way behind God's back!*

As the last of the warm relaxing bush tea courses through her body, Ma Jo Jo reasons that worrying over something in which she has no control would only raise her blood pressure, so she begins to breathe slowly and deeply once again, pushing away any disconcerting thoughts and focusing instead on tomorrow, Sunday, the day after the storm.

Having again moved out of the kitchen, she stands in the doorway looking proudly at the highly polished dining table. She's thinking of the women who like her, earlier in the day, might have been with rag and O'cedar furniture polish in hand, bringing out the brilliance and luster of their tables and other furniture. The usual Saturday chores of most of the village wives or their teenage daughters.

Ma Jo Jo snickers at the knowledge that in these homes, no one will sit at those tables but perchance the man of the house chooses to have his customary late Sunday lunch at the table, he certainly would do so but not before the missus throws a tablecloth over its shining surface.

Ma Jo Jo, finished with admiring her highly polished table, backs away and heads to the kitchen to her lowly plain wooden kitchen table. She ignores the two straight back chairs on opposite ends and pulls out the wooden bench beneath it. She plops down and immediately draws up one leg, laying it out fully on the bench. She bends over, studying her swollen ankles, timidly poking at them. Flinching in pain, she spontaneously withdraws her fingers.

Ma Jo Jo is angry with herself; she doesn't need this injury with the approaching storm. If only she had let the mother hen be, to lay her eggs and then hatch her brood or whatever she was doing, in the box under the house.

Chapter 7

The gusty and mournful cries of the winds coming up from deep down in the valley and rushing through the quivering trees around ma Jo Jo's house, sitting at the incline of the hill, had lulled her into a fitful sleep. But now the loud music coming from the Irish woman's gramophone has jolted her wide awake. She gets up from the bench and painfully limps into her bedroom, positioning herself in front of the window with the largest cracks, where she can see clearly up the hill to the Irishwoman's house.

Since the death of her husband, the plainly reclusive woman but to the villagers, *eccentric* woman, has taken her eccentricity to another level where her music is concerned. She now plays only two records from her vast collection; of the two played over and over, one is about this Irish fishmonger girl from Dublin, the other about this errant fair-haired soldier boy, who is about to die. Hanged, shot maybe?

Ma Jo Jo now recalls that those records had been eerily screeching from *'foreday morning'*, very early before the break of dawn. The one about the fair-haired boy, seemed even more haunting and painful today. Nevertheless, she begins to wordlessly mouth the words of the song. *"A fair – haired boy in a foreign land at sunrise was to die. In a prison cell he sat alone... the reason none could say... A tear, a sigh, a sad goodbye... the pardon came too late."* Ma Jo Jo trails off, not remembering all of the song or who sang it. She feels it coming from deep within her wretched soul, the tears that would often come gushing out, washing over but never would cleanse or heal her. The fair-haired boy did not have to die! Just like she did not have to *'die'* over 40 years ago!

Ma Jo Jo cannot take it anymore, the song. She is about to take her hands to her ears to block out the sounds of her own pitiful wails, but thankfully the record has come to a screeching yet merciful end. Guess, the fair – haired boy is riddled with bullets or swinging at the end of a rope now, ah well!

Ma Jo Jo smiles cynically as the Irish woman puts on the other record and cranks up the volume which is competing with the earth-shattering thunder rolls and loud piercing rain on her ceiling – less tin roof.

'In Dublin fair city where the girls are so pretty, I just set my eyes on sweet Molly Malone; as she wheels her wheelbarrow, through the streets broad and narrow, crying cockles and mussels alive, alive oh!' The singer croons on. *"So, de Irish woman is in dat frame of mind, eh?"* Ma Jo Jo questions, as she swoons behind her close board window. She is not aware that she is swooning and now swaying on her swollen ankles – the slight twinges of pain she is ignoring.

The series of air splitting thunder rolls compounded with the angry howling winds breathing their cold deathly breaths through every crack of her wooden house, caressing an wrapping themselves like cold icy blankets around her, are cutting Ma Jo Jo off from the Irish woman and pretty Molly Malone – the fishmonger from Dublin; alive alive oh!

Ma Jo Jo begins to sway as she dreamingly slips back into her past, her youth... She's there on the stage belting out her Sarah Vaughn and Josephine Baker songs ... ... Isn't that handsome young man at the back of the hall with the Panama hat shading his face; he who is trying to be conspicuous, her Joseph Celestine?

Josephine would know him anywhere, she giggles wickedly. Trying to hide from her, is he; He, the center of her world? She decides to tease him. She bursts out with a sweet **'lavway'**. Yes, she belts out a sweet made up song on the spot, accompanied by her **'dingolaying'**, her dancing as they would do when *'playing de fool'* down by the river. Hands and feet in fleeting and frenzied movements, with the waterfall roaring above them, then crashing down murderously on the rocks drowning out their loud and lustily singing voices. Their audience, the fowls of the air and the few that might have wandered away from backyards or their coops to scratch at the moist earth of the riverbank for food.

On these occasions Joseph and Josephine would end up collapsing in each other's arms laughing with hilarity still singing their ribald song at the top of their voices, knowing that no one could, and sometimes not even they would hear themselves, not with the thunderous waterfall as their cover .

Now Ma Jo Jo continues the trend, lustily singing the latest ribald calypso and telling its story with her seductive hand movements. But wait why does he have such a revolting look on his face? Why is he backing away, now fleeing from her?

~~~

The anguished Ma Jo Jo is choking on the sobs that she is determined not be released. If Pa Joe Joe is up there looking down disapprovingly on her – she would not give him the satisfaction of seeing her tears – wasted tears. She realizes now that she was just trying to remake their history. She knows that the older Joseph and the barely just out of her teens Josephine, would never have displayed such lasciviousness on the banks of the river. Make over their life indeed! She quickly removes her hands from her thickened waist and they involuntary pass over her ample hips – she cringes in disgust.

Ma Jo Jo is firmly jolted back to the present on hearing a cacophony of voices hurrying pass her house, heading for the hills. She quickly steps back to the window from which her dancing feet had taken her away. Again, she peers through its cracks, her eyes searching the backs of the scurrying forms that she cannot recognize. The rains that have been pouring for hours now, giving their rain hats and coats quite the beating, as they scamper up the hill, slipping and sliding all the way.

Ma Jo Jo's eyes scans the hill, trying to see through the sheets of rain and madly falling branches of the trees that are being bowed and at the mercy of the elements that are now part of the yet to arrive, destructive storm.
~~~

Ma Jo Jo espies the illuminated lantern on the Irish woman's bannister. She wonders at its steadfastness; It not yet toppled over by the furious winds and *'pelting'* rains. Then she sees the brightest of lights ever in someone's home, coming from beyond the Irish woman's gallery, inside the living room. She gives a little laugh and shakes her head at the knowledge that the Irish woman still wears her little sweaters that she brought with her from Dublin Ireland and also has a fireplace which she often *feeds*, complaining that here, up high in the mountains it's always chilly in the evenings and early mornings.

Ma Jo Jo let's a brittle little laugh escape her lips at the idea of the Irish woman calling their little, *'lil'* hill a mountain. Then after going back and forth with herself on the difference between a hill and a mountain, Ma Jo Jo finally concludes that while the hill was not *'lil'*, it certainly was not a mountain.

Suddenly panicked, she throws open wide her broad window. There is no way she could see the small flickering fire in the Irish woman's fireplace. The rising crescendo of voices coming from the people going up the hill, causes Ma Jo Jo to climb atop a stool to get a better view.

At first, disbelieving what her eyes are seeing, Ma Jo Jo quickly comes to the realization that what she thought was the lantern on her banister was not so. The reality; The Irish woman with the flaming red hair, her house is on fire! It's up in flames, bright orange flames!

The Irish woman who got a telegram three days ago, letting her know that her beloved mother had died two days prior; That Irish woman who misses her husband something terrible, that Irish woman who has stated plainly to anyone who would listen, that she doesn't feel the need to live anymore, that woman's house is on fire! Alive alive oh!

The fire, beautiful tongues of orange flames are reaching up to the heavens as if in prayer but yet are contained in the inferno that was once the neat and tidy Irish woman's house. The storm being no respecter of persons or things, not even the roaring pretty fire, dumps a deluge, quickly extinguishing it. Yep, the big bad storm does.

Ma Jo Jo clears her throat, this she does again, *"em hmm!"* she says empathetically and shudders. "So be it", she mutters still at the window. She's watching the now thick black smoke of the fire ravaged house, rising above the trees.

"She died of a fever... and that was the end of sweet Molly Malone ... Now her ghost wheels her wheelbarrow through the streets broad and narrow ... Crying cockles and mussels alive alive oh. Alive, alive oh, oh! Alive oh, oh!" "hmmm!" Ma Jo Jo continues the song though butchering most of it, not hearing the record to sing along with; "hmmm!" she says deep in thought. Now she remembers the singers of the song, "The Dubliners! The Dubliners!" she cries out aloud. Maybe she would get the record one day, when in the city. She giggles hitting herself upside her head, now where is she going to play the record, she not having the gramophone that most of the villagers were probably now owning.

Ma Jo Jo starts again... *"In Dublin fair city where the girls are so pretty, I once knew a girl..."* Ma Jo Jo pauses, only now realizing that she never knew the Irish woman's name. *"Alive alive oh, Alive alive oh, singing cockles and mussels alive alive oh!"* Ma Jo Jo continues in tribute to the woman "Em hmm!" Ma Jo Jo once more says with conviction and closes the window.

She looks down at the big puddle on the floor; She doesn't have to touch her bed to know that it has suffered a good soaking too. The cause, her now discovered leaking roof! *"Singing cockles and mussels alive alive oh!"*

Chapter 8

Ma Jo Jo steps in front of her bureau peering nervously into its mirror as if for the first time. Where did the years go? Ma Jo Jo is looking and thinking of her *'collapsing'* body. Her thickened waist and more than ample hips. Did Pa Joe Joe notice these changes too? Was that one of the reasons he begged her to stop loving him and move on?

Ma Jo Jo grimaces at her feeble attempt to evade the truth of their destroyed life. Her arms are lying protectively across her chest, her head lying in the crock of her neck. She's rocking her body to and fro, hoping that for just a few moments, she could rock away her ever present guilty feelings; The part she played in the young Joseph Celestine's destroyed life.

Ma Jo Jo tightly closes her eyes and begins to sing aloud; Still, she can clearly see the blood spurting high up in the air, then falling back down as rain, in clumps, soiling the beautiful green grass.

Ma Jo Jo Is screaming out the words of the song. She is seeing the Older One playing on the green grass that she had painstakingly planted in front of her house. The greenest and *'prettiest'* in the neighborhood, was everyone's consensus.

Ma Jo Jo sees that Pa Joe Joe is peeping at her and the Older One at play, there on the beautiful green grass, from behind the drawing room curtains. Then darkness! Pa Joe Joe is at the lawn with his hoe, he's digging at it! The clumps of grass and earth are going way up to the sky, then turning into clumps of mud as they hit the ground. The Older One is crying out for him to stop it, to stop hurting the beautiful green grass!

Ma Jo Jo is aghast, she wants to stop him for the crying Older One's sake but she can't, she won't, because it's her fault, everything is her fault! The tears are streaming down the Older Ones cheeks, she's pulling and tugging at Ma Jo Jo's flared skirt, urging her to go across to Pa Joe Joe, to stop him from hurting the beautiful grass but Ma Jo Jo just can't.

Bawling out her hurt, the Older One turns and runs away. Ma Jo Jo Looks at the little legs running away, scampering up the hill as fast as they could go – to her refuge, where she would stay from thence forth.

Ma Z had heard the commotion and is already out the door waiting to scoop the traumatized child into her arms.

Pa Joe Joe momentarily stops his hoeing, his eyes following the fleeing child up the hill. For a second his cold eyes meet with that of Ma Z's; the frigidity between them like a silent deadly moving iceberg.

Pa Joe Joe is hoeing away, digging way down deep, even deeper than the roots of the grass that offends him so, as if to make sure that nothing now, not even a single blade of the offending grass would ever see the light of day, ever again. Leaving the yard an unsightly mess and the neighbors astonished at what had become of the most beautiful lawn in the neighborhood. They, the neighbors, are sympathetically understanding to Pa Joe Joe, like him they too, would never forget, though they have moved on.

~~~

Ma Jo Jo knows that she should stop this nonsense immediately. This uselessness of slipping back into the past, "Please, please not at a time like this," she begs, cautioning herself, but in spite of the gentle admonishment Ma Jo Jo has gone back, yet again, way way back...

'Joseph Celestine's Athleticism Knows No Bounds,' screams the headlines of the most read newspaper in the island 'scholarship scholarship!' its rivals demanded. He had vanquished all his
~~~

opponents in every event he participated, at the just completed sporting competition abroad.

...The island, the village in particular is awash with excitement. The villagers are giddy and drunk with excitement, both literally and figuratively. The policemen are turning their heads away today, from all the little *'hiccups'* this excitement is causing. He is making his triumphant return to the island, to his, *'their'* village today. He is *'theirs'*, the villagers – he belongs to them!

The celebrants under the *eve* of the Chineseman's shop, the shaded awning, openly guzzle the beers that are not supposed to be sold on a Sunday... The Lord's Day. The *'don't give a damn ones'*, the really daring ones, are taking shots of the illegally distilled bottle of *'babash'* or other bush rum, in brown paper bags; no sneaking away to the bushes today.

Today they are celebrating their hero, their 'village boy', period! He has put the island on the map, the world's athletic map. Soon the buses, the fan hired buses, will be arriving to take them to the airport to welcome *'their boy'* back home.

The excitement under the *eve* of the shop is growing. Every now and again, one of the men whose wrist is adorned with a watch, more of a vanity item, since the good ol' sun and its shadow, lends for a good and accurate time telling.

The Chineseman is behind the counter of his shop, his customary wide grin plastered on his face is even wider today. He is catching a welcomed break from his loyal customers wicked good-natured shouts, in changing his name to Mr. Chin, Mr. Chong or Mr. Chow, knowing fully well that his name is just plain 'Mr. Bill.'

He too, the Chineseman is caught up in the excitement of the impending return of the village hero, Joseph Celestine. He is telling everyone that he has known him since he was a *'Lil, Lil'* fellow and would on occasions freely give him some *'paradise plums'* or a *'Kaiser Ball'* too. The one large Kaiser Ball candy, being the equivalent of two paradise plum candies.

The Chineseman looks behind at his near empty shelves. His sometimes helper, the village drunk, had just four hours ago replenished the shelves. The Chineseman's brows furrows with interest; Something of every item was being sold. Even the cans with near expiration dates that he was contemplating of pulling off the shelves and sending back to the wholesalers in the city were being sold, ah well!

The Chineseman flexes his small but taut muscles and goes to the door, hoping to draw the attention of his helper, from the midst of this happy but raucous crowd. As if this is possible, the Chineseman's grin is spreading even wider as he decides to join the revelers whenever they returned from the airport, with the village hero. He would close the shop and donate cases of *'sweet drinks'*, those new flavored sodas that were not doing quite so well. He thinks again and decides against that move. He certainly does not wish to be called a scamp today. He would mix those slow sellers with the favorites of the villagers. Later on, they would remember his generosity and drop the *'scamp'* moniker that some would good naturedly shout at him, but which would often rankle him.

Suddenly his eyes opens up wide with excitement, the familiar grin still plastered on his face. He knows what he will *'put on'*, he would certainly wear that *hot* red shirt, the one with the big bold yellow hibiscus flowers, that Ma Z had given him as a Christmas gift. *"Wear it for de carnival celebration"*, she had encouraged when she saw the look of uncertainty on his face. Today's celebration is as good as any for wearing the shirt, which he never thought that he would ever wear.

Mr. Bill waves across the man, his helper, who of course is *'high'*, near drunk. After they restock the shelves he would get dressed and then go and join the *'lime'*, the celebration with his new friends. Mr. Bill giggles and giggles, his bony shoulders shaking uncontrollably on his decision to leave the door of his shop open 'just a crack', perchance a reveler would want to purchase something.

~~~

The men are in their *"Sunday Best"* their bright colored cotton shirts starched and pressed, their pants seams *"cutting"*. Their *'kick and stab'*, their shoes polished and brilliantly shining. Those
~~~

occasionally worn *'pointy tipped shoes'*, now out of their boxes and peeping out from beneath the hems of linen and flannel pants, which most of them seem, unfortunately to be sweeping the ground.

Today the gym boots, crepe soles and watchicongs, those lower level footwear would be 'taking a rest', definitely not be worn... Big grown men are heading northeast today! Not one of those snooty nosed city folks would be looking down on them today, and derisively thinking that the *'country boukies'* had come to town.

Today, they are on an even playing field – they, the generous villagers were going to *'share their boy'* with the whole island. Yes, he is theirs, who has brought glory to the whole island but would be leaving to go back to the village with them, his people. There would be no overnighting in the city; repairing to any fancy hotel. The rest of his people were anxiously awaiting his arrival back in the village to welcome him their way. No big *'sawatee'*, *'big pappy'*, moralistic speaking government official, would thwart their celebration. If they want to celebrate the village's hero, then they should come up to the village!

Today, the so called *'country boukies'* would not be made to feel out of place and inferior. They may not know how to *bump*, *grind* or *swagga* like those flamboyantly dressed *'saga boys'*; those aptly named showboats from the city and towns. Today, the world is their oyster; their boy Joseph Celestine is coming home with a bucket full of medals.

Back in the village, the motor car with the loudspeaker atop, had been to all the tracks and traces, even the steep hills, announcing the celebration to be held later. Joseph Celestine their athletic hero was coming 'home' after he deplaned.

~~~

In the airport, the announcement that the best beating steel band in the land would be serenading the incoming victorious athletic team, has the crowd screaming with excitement. In fact, they are already here *'knocking up'* their pans, yes, warming up the steel drums. The waving gallery and curiously, the arrival hall are
~~~

teeming with people. How they got into the hall is good a guess as any, it being only used for arriving passengers.

Hopefully, the security guards will not be sent to enforce their stringent laws on a day like this; put a damper on things. The villagers have just arrived in the four chartered buses, every last seat accounted for.

They, the villagers are now beginning to grasp the enormity of *'this thing'*, what the triumph of Joseph Celestine and his team means to the whole island. That they, the villagers, are really just small fishes in a very large pond in which they are now floundering, in which they are being swallowed up by the massive crowd that has turned out to see *'their hero'*, the boy from the *'country'*.

The villagers should have expected this; On nearing the airport both sides of the street are lined with people, some waving posters with his picture plastered thereon; yet others waving the flag of the country. Some were shouting out the name of Joseph Celestine, whenever a vehicle or bicyclist passes by. The people are *'kicksing off'*, just having fun, until the real entourage of Joseph Celestine comes into view. Very grudgingly, the villagers, the 'Country Boukies' have come to the realization, that their boy is not theirs alone anymore, that the whole of the island has rightly claimed him too.

The plane having landed and taxiing along the runway has brought out a deafening roar from the crowd. The steel band men in their colorful nylon shirts are pounding away on their instruments and jumping up to their own infectious music. The long beautiful plumes certainly not found in any of the birds around and stuck in their straw hats are swaying effortlessly with their dance moves. The crowds that were previously contained in the waving gallery and arrival hall now seems to be bursting at their seams.

This cannot be happening! From among the steel band, out pops the most beloved calypsonian in the land, in the world! With a devilish grin on his face! He's dancing toward the forefront of the steel band. Yes! Yes! Yes! The door of the plane is opening up; there he is Joseph! Joseph! Joseph! The crowd is going wild. But wait, those bodies coming over the banister of the waving gallery, are they being pushed or voluntarily jumping over? Five, six, seven bodies are being counted; Three are up and running toward the plane.

The crowd is egging them on, encouraging them to outrun the security guards with their upheld batons in hand. Two of them are brought down by the might of the guards. The waves of boisterous cheers, the support from the crowd, is propelling the lone survivor forward!

He has made it to the fourth step of the plane; panting and grasping at his chest. It is *'Big Ches'*, the friend of Joseph Celestine, who is now standing there on the platform of the plane, one hand folded across his chest, the other playing with the newly sprouted stubble on his chin, that he is so proud of.

Joseph is sure that on seeing his stubble, his father would jokingly warn him that this does not allow him to start playing *'mannish'*... that he would still have to bend his back and sweep the yard with his cocoyea broom and feed the animals too!

Joseph is looking down on his panting friend, and shakes his head in disbelief at what his best friend had just pulled off, an embarrassing smile on his face but his eyes full of love and admiration. Looking up at him Big Ches' straightens up and heaves his shoulders as if to say, *"Ah done it again, do suppen embarrassing!"*

Now, Joseph doubles up in laughter, the crowd doing likewise, roaring with approval. 'Big Ches' looks down, smiling at the security guards; at the one panting and holding his chest too. The crowd previously howling with laughter, has now erupted in boos as another guard joins in; in an attempt to go after 'Big Ches' who is quickly ascending a few more steps of the plane.

The tense situation is lightened as Joseph Celestine himself, with some officials and other athletes behind him, descends the stairs and embraces his friend Big Ches', taking him down the stairs – his hand extended across his shoulders. The two winded yet sterned faced baton wielding security guards trailing after them.

The steel band men had not stopped beating on their pans or dancing, even the calypsonian who has not as yet uttered one word of his calypso, is doing his gyrations as is his custom. The crowd has once again erupted with chants of Joseph! Joseph! Joseph! at the direction of the calypsonian now with the mic in one of his hands, and a baton in the other.

~~~

Ma Jo Jo has once again devolved in howls, now that her ruminations of her Joseph Celestine, is back to where they belong, sent back to what she calls her regrettable past. Ma Jo Jo howls are competing with those of the howling and raging winds outside.

She was there too, at the airport being one of the few young women on the bus, who were given permission by their mothers. The fathers having no say in anything of that nature pertaining to their daughters. He was her Joseph, her hero; hers more so than anyone else's – or was he ever?

Ma Jo Jo is miserable, no longer in control, she has now become one with the atmospherics outside her house. She is part of the maelstrom that is visiting the village and its humble people – they don't deserve this.

Ma Jo Jo is sure that her howls can be heard above the malevolent winds that surely must be ripping apart the village at this time. Suddenly she stops with her howling, hoping that the old woman above her, higher up the hill has not heard her. Ma Jo Jo swears that, even if she does and comes down to her on a night like this, the old woman would be ignored. Now Ma Jo Jo is doubly miserable, why did she allow the old woman into her thoughts? Does she think that because Pa Joe Joe is no longer around, gone two weeks now... Ma Jo Jo would just not use the right term for Pa Joe Joe's absence from the village.

Ma Jo Jo is wracked with tears of grief, her shoulders shaking uncontrollably. For the past two weeks she has been involuntarily reliving the most wretched parts of her last forty years. Why did she let thoughts of the old woman pervade her space? Does she think that she would allow her back into her life – she who represents the main part of their ruined life?
~~~

Ma Jo Jo is gratified that her now deep controlled sobs have replaced the howls, that had been ripping through every nerve and fiber of her being. She lifts up the end of her very wide skirt and sops up the tears running down her cheeks. She straightens up thinking; maybe, maybe, if they survive the storm, the old woman and her, maybe they could build ...Ma Jo Jo starts to howl again, thoughts of the old woman the night before comes crashing into her ...

~~~

The old woman quickly slips out of her house, carefully descending the steps, at the same time thinking that most of the houses in the village, with their cleanly swept yards have one thing in common; unsafe steps. The old woman with her long and bulky cotton *'nightie'* hauled up in one hand and the other holding down the hastily wrapped head tie – there to protect her head from the falling dew.

She was abruptly awakened from her sleep – she wasn't sure if it was a deep one or not. All she knows is that for the past two weeks this has been a nightly occurrence, her being jolted awake. Then, quickly as she could, slips off her bed nervously slipping her feet in the *'sapats'* at the front of her bed.

For far too many nights, she has been hearing the different tones of Ma Jo Jo's screams, not to know when she is desperately needed – only if she would relent and let her inside her house is another matter. She knows that Ma Jo Jo has to let go of her perceived hatred of her and start their healing. She hurries past the little houses where the lamp lights are being turned on and the lamps thrusted out the doorways to illuminate her path downhill. They too, the neighbors have heard Ma Jo Jo's painful shouts – have been hearing them night after night, for the past two weeks.

Ma Z keeps her head hung low, she needs not meet the eyes of the *'clucking'* tongued women, those similarly head ties wearing women – they can keep their sympathetic noises. *"Ent none of dem business, none of dem pain but Josephine and mines,"* she would add
~~~

defiantly scampering down the hill to the outside of Ma Jo Jo's bedroom, beating on its wooden walls, begging to be let in.

The men, they have been hearing Ma Jo Jo's nightly howls too, but unlike the women, would not unwind their comfortably wrapped bodies from the coarse cotton coverlets, that's been skillfully made by their wives, from flour sacks purchased from the Chineseman's shop for a few twenty – five cent pieces. The sacks washed by being pounded on stones by the river, then washed again before being laid out on nearby bushes to be dried before being transformed into the snugly covers that the men would wrap themselves in at night.

No, the men would not roll out of bed – besides, Ma Jo Jo's almost nightly screams, were women's business, they will deal with that, they the men would only get in the way. Furthermore, years ago it was firmly established that they had taken a side. Funny how things did not change one bit after all these years; they were still on Joseph Celestine's side.

Through the years as time went by, everyone in the village looked on uncomfortably as their once thought of hero, to the sporting world, aged and diminished in stature. This was not supposed to be the outcome of Joseph Celestine!

His cold indifference to Josephine and the perceived *'pressure'* that he put her through the last forty years, were of no concern of theirs. She and more so the old woman, destroyed him and the village's hope of ever gaining glory. Not one iota of blame was placed on Mr. Leo, the village's benefactor from the early years. Therefore, the nearly nightly guttural screams emanating from deep within Ma Jo Jo's tortured soul these past two weeks, would not rouse these men from off their beds. ***Her conscience is eating she alive***, they had already determined.

The women, their lamps and lanterns thrust outside, illuminating her way downhill, their quiet shouts of fear and warnings, even their whispered words of comfort to the old woman were studiously avoided. Hypocrites! Were her thoughts of them all.

Resignedly, one by one the women would douse their lights, close their doors and creep back into their beds and into the comforting arms of their husbands, a place where Ma Jo Jo was not destined to be. They would hear but could not help her but Ma Jo Jo's near nightly screams have helped them, drawing these women closer to their husbands, not only in their arms but closer into their hearts and lives.

The old woman is furiously beating on Ma Jo Jo's door, her pleas to be let in, to comfort her is being ignored – what the old woman would really like Ma Jo Jo to do, is to let her into her life once again. She moves to the back of Ma Jo Jo's bedroom where the wailing is suddenly more pronounced, Ma Jo Jo having moved there to completely ignore her pleas to be let in.

The old woman has unwrapped her head, freeing it from the constrictions of the headtie that is now trailing behind her on the soggy ground. She repositions herself at the door of the living room where Ma Jo Jo has once again moved, to avoid her. The old woman repeatedly stomps a foot in frustration. **"May I ketch a cold tonite an' die!"** the old woman dramatically wishes upon herself.

Many years ago, most of the villagers had wished that upon her too, **death**! But she could not succumb to their wishes, to the shame and the blame of what had befallen Joseph Celestine and Josephine. She refused to become a living dead, a zombie like Josephine. She had to fight off the blame, the guilt that the villagers had laid at her feet – as a matter of fact, she never felt any of those things.

The old woman looks at her bleeding hands, she has been pounding away something fiercely at the roughly hewn wood of Ma Jo Jo's door. With determination she balls her fists and raises them to strike at the door again but they are swollen and painful. She bites into her lips, the pain so fierce, the movements she cannot complete. Thankfully, the screams and gut-wrenching wails from within the room has somewhat subsided – just her quiet sobs can now be heard through the cracks of the wooden walls. The old woman, her face pressed against the rough boards, is whispering comforting words, urging Ma Jo Jo to let go of Pa Joe Joe, that it was so long ago – let him go. Yes, it was over such a long, long time ago, not just the two weeks ago when he was placed in the ground – let him go, it is finished! *"Josephine, I love yuh!"* The woman whispers in anguish. She does not wait for a reply of the angry scream she knows would be forthcoming as she gives up and scrambles up the hill to her home in the dark night.

<center>~~~</center>

Ma Jo Jo finds herself once again in front of the wagonette – dancing. She is trying to pick up from where she had left off hours ago but try as she might, her performance is lackluster, pathetically so, even though she is putting everything into it; gesticulating wildly, prancing around, her movements are reeking of frustration and fooling no one but herself. Ma Jo Jo gives up – she must not fool herself anymore there was no gaiety in her past, her childhood yes, but no cause for dancing or celebrating the now.

The sudden bumps on her house and thunder rolls high above, have brought the highly anxious Ma Jo Jo down a notch or two. She heaves her shoulders in defeat. She had already taken all the precautions that she could against this upcoming monster of a storm. It was, just three days ago that the annoying so-called weather officials perused the village in their car, outfitted with loudspeakers atop, blasting out the news of this upcoming, never before experienced monster storm.

The villagers thought of them as nuisances, they, doing their broadcasting even late at night. Late at night to most villagers, meant that the sun had slipped away with the moon slyly creeping in to take its place and the darkness as if by magic, descending on the village, the board windows and doors being quietly shuttered – it being after 6:00 PM.

Now, with some more disturbances on her roof, Ma Jo Jo begins to feel her anger rising; Anger at herself because after hopefully securing the roofs of her pig pens and fowl coops, Elvin and his friends had come by inquiring if their services might be needed but she gently assured them that she was OK. She was quite fed up with the constant pounding on the roofs of the houses around her; "Pounding! Pounding! Pounding!" In fact, for the past few days this seem to be the only activity happening in the neighborhood – pounding! Hammers and nails coming down unmercifully on tin and galvanized roofs. She was quite sick of it! Now, with the avocados falling indiscriminately on her roof and their branches falling or sweeping her roof with every gust of wind she wishes that she was not so dismissive of those concerned young men, and hired them to trim some of the low hanging branches.

Ma Jo Jo hands **'flies'** to her head as she hears the earsplitting crash on her roof. She imagines that the house has just been shaken to its foundation and swear that this time it is not only the branches but the whole zaboca tree has fallen on the roof.

Again, if only she had paid Elvin and his friends the few dollars that they would have charged her to pick the fruit off the laden branches and cut those low hanging branches directly over her roof. Ma Jo Jo Shakes her head and lets out a shrill frustrated cry. It was not about the money – she was just about had it with the storm. **Lordy** if only Pa Joe Joe was still here, Ma Jo Jo muses. He would have taken charge; she would not have to be upset about a few zabocas or their branches falling on her roof or even of that old dead bird still lying on the living room floor.

She shivers at the thought of the bird and sneaks a peek into the now darkened room, puzzling at the darkness. Isn't the lamp supposed to be aglow? She having filled it with kerosene just two days ago.

She is making her signature series of low sighs because she has unknowingly given into her musings once again. Pa Joe Joe is not in her life anymore. Yet another truth, he had been gone since that fateful day of her farewell concert. To be sure, that brooding figure that returned five years later to open his church was not the one who had left her lying there on the previously green grass, entangle between the tall weeds and bushes, taking her soul with him as he left her there, with the badly wounded Mr. Leo.

Everyone was surprised when he came back to her, surmising in the end, that he was only doing so to exact his pound of flesh, to punish her for her perceived sin against him, but the moment when he did lay his eyes on her again, the five years of bitterness, self-torture and planned revenge all but vanished in a cloud of forgiveness. Yet he could not take her or have her in his arms. The picture of her, of 'them', lying entangled between the bushes was indelibly stamped in his mind – no, he must never forget, or forgive her!

Pa Joe Joe could not forget, not even from the pulpit was he safe from his thoughts. The day his life was curtailed would play over and over in his mind. Seeing his Josephine lying there, trembling in unimaginable terror, totally pushed him to commit 'the act', then he ran away. He didn't touch her, couldn't, thinking, maybe never again.

The young Joseph Celestine ran and ran screaming in unmitigated terror and anger. His blinding rage and the sudden ominous hurricane like winds whipping at his back, propelling him forward, faster than his athletic legs would normally take him – straight to where his adversary was awaiting him, sitting patiently atop the wide open gates of hell; his home for the choosing.

~~~

Now Ma Jo Jo's sobs are wracking her body, the sobs again turning into heart rending never before heard screams, then into quiet moans. As if on cue, the lamp lights are being reluctantly turned on in the wooden one and two bedroom homes around hers – her larger one. The occupants of these homes are quite fed up with Ma Jo Jo's now nightly outbursts, most putting down these outbursts to her guilty conscience for what she had done too Pa Joe Joe, essentially destroying him.

Those who did not share these sentiments said nothing, less they'd be thought of as traitors and though concerned, they never scampered over to her during her nightly primal and heart tugging wails, to comfort her. She did not need them, she would have screamed at them if they did come, couldn't they understand that her life – Pa Joe Joe was gone? Now let her grieve in peace!

Ma Jo Jo can't or won't stop going back in time, way, way, back to yet another incident. Pa Joe Joe has just rappelled down the coconut tree, faster than he intended, with a bunch of the nuts entangle between him and his safety rope. Ma Jo Jo makes as if to
~~~

go to his aid. Pa Joe Joe now aground, simply waves her away with the cutlass which he pulls from its sheath, fastened around his waist and begins to deftly shave off the tops of the water nuts, then pour the water into the enamel mug that Ma Jo Jo has offered up.

Ma Jo Jo's eyes are drawn to the tarantula that is about to climb onto the fold of his pant legs. She screams out, at the same time dropping the mug of coconut water in her hands. Pa Joe Joe agilely steps aside, crushing the insect under his boot. Wide eyed she looks up at him; she, trembling and afraid also. Is she reading too much in the strange, cold and angry look in his eyes? She has become sorely afraid of him the love of her life – but how could that be? He in turn is looking down, into those terrified troubled eyes. Is this what his lost years have done to them, to her? Pa Joe Joe feels a surge of guilt, compassion too, flooding his entire body. He begins to feel this warm glow flowing from his heart straight into his loins. He could feel the cracking of the wall of ice around his heart, the crumbling of that wall, as the icy cold waters roars over what remains of the steel walls standing between them. Pa Joe Joe drops the cutlass now burning into his hand, suddenly realizing that everything he touched and used, even his words, he weaponized against her – against them.

He does not have to draw her into his arms, she is there even before the cutlass hits the ground. Then, he encircles her with those two powerful arms, drawing her in even closer, crushing her against his chest. Ma Jo Jo feels his racing heart, his pulsating pelvic area. She can hardly breathe, twitch a muscle, but she won't make a move. She dares not spoil this crazy moment; she had waited five years for him to come home to her.

Ma Jo Jo feels herself being lifted off the ground, higher and higher. Now he lowers her a bit, he's smothering her face with wet hungry kisses. He pauses abruptly, looks deep into her eyes and gently, ever so gently he brings her down to the ground, drawing her deep into him, whispering to her all the silly things that he'd whispered to her before, causing her to laugh out hysterically – the silly young man! Now he remembers, doesn't he?

Ma Jo Jo is on cloud nine. He is again making promises that he made to her in their youth, those that would make her feel peaceful and protected. Ma Jo Jo smiles blissfully as Pa Joe Joe lifts her up again, high up above him once more. He, once before would have done so unsteadily, ungainly even, though never would he have let her fall. Surely his five years of lifting weights would have seen to that. His thrusting her way up in the air is sure – he is also looking into her eyes seeing the pain and hurt that he has brought her.

Pa Joe Joe realizes that the carefree giddy laughter isn't coming out, isn't there anymore. Really, what did he do to her? He looks away and shakes his head in exasperation – he wasn't sure that he could heal the hurting – the deep wide wounds. He grits his teeth *"geesanages!"* He doesn't even know if he wants to stop hurting her now, in essence, punishing her!

He gently let's her down, pull her in real close once more and begins to croon their favorite Sarah Vaughn song of the past. In fact, that was supposed to be the song that she was about to sing in that crowded village hall the day their world came to a bloody end.

Now, suddenly he thrusts her back up in the air. Wishing to block out that memory that refuses to leave him; That would torture him each and every one of those five excruciating years that he was away from her. Destroying his soul. Yes, even on becoming a preacher, healing and saving lost souls, he could do nothing for himself.

Through the dense cluster of trees, Ma Jo Jo is looking at the fading sun slinking away. She is becoming aware of Pa Joe Joe's increasingly tight grip on her still slim waist. Like a vice his fingers are digging into her flesh – holding onto her for dear life, begging her to save him, them, from him. At this moment, Ma Jo Jo could save neither of them because she too has begun her own fight. Her chance of happiness is being dashed for the second time since he's back, and again on a Sunday under the coconut tree. She's hearing the slow sliding of the iron bolt on the bottom half of the wooden door. It is the child known as the Older One. Ma Jo Jo is determined to ignore that her second chance of happiness could be curtailed by the Older One opening that door; she is going to focus on their brief but happy past ...

Ma Jo Jo is giggling like a schoolgirl in love, being held up high under the shady swaying branches of the coconut tree by her Joseph

Celestine. Then, those tiny feet that she often pretends to eat, the toes that she loves to nibble on, just to hear the Older One screech in happiness, is coming closer and closer to crush her chance at happiness yet again. The toes are nervously digging into the dusty yard, hesitantly working their way forward. The bearer, ignoring Ma Jo Jo's gesticulations That she should back away, not to come closer, putting an end to the possibilities, and therefore continuing the nightmare that is her present life.

Ma Jo Jo's look is silently pleading to the Older One – whose one hand is playing with her fibrous uncombed hair, the other, over her mouth, trying to stifle her nervous giggles as she looks at Ma Jo Jo whom she imagines is scared of being held up in the sky by Pa Joe Joe.

Pa Joe Joe feigns weakness of arms and Ma Jo Jo unwittingly screams out. The child too, screams out, running up to Pa Joe Joe, trembling with rage and lashing out – pounding again and again on his legs with her tiny balled up fists, as the tears stream down her cheeks. Pa Joe Joe looks on with pain filled eyes, as Ma Jo Jo now on her knees, scoops the child into her arms, gently shushing her.

There in the dust, Pa Joe Joe kneels down beside the two tragic figures and hugs them tightly. He would like to tell them that from now on things will be alright; That he loves them both and would protect and care for them but he knows that these words playing in his head, could never leave his lips. Instead he gets up from the dusty ground and walks away. Ma Jo Jo watches as he walks away and holds onto the child even tighter. She knows exactly where he is heading and how things are about to unfold with him.

~~~

Pa Joe Joe breaks into a sprint as he heads to the river, cutting through the bushes – because of his frenzied and sprinted pace, the tall grasses are cutting at his arms, his chest, his whole body – the blood flowing immediately. His white sleeveless merino offering no protection as it too, soon becomes shredded and blood soaked. He is running to the stream along the man-made gutters that would take him deep into the forest and up the steep hill that would
~~~

ultimately lead him to the gigantic rock, high above the waterfall, where in his youth he would go and nestled in its cleft, where he would find the peace to calm his troubled soul.

Pa Joe Joe, once more is transformed into the young athletic Joseph Celestine. He's hearing the wild applause of the village crowd. He, hurdling over the bamboo bar; With a short sprinted run, the bamboo pole in his hand, his make believe javelin is thrown and quivers in the air as it passes the others thrown; his, landing at a distance that no other competitor matches. The crowd, the village is in a festive mood – lifting him high on their collective shoulders. **'Dey Boy'**, has once again, outperformed the competition from the surrounding villages!

Pa Joe Joe is looking up at his sacred celestial throne above the waterfall. The cleft in the grand rock, is beckoning him to come hither, to sit on his throne, his rightfully, which no other in his youth, would dare try to inhabit. Not after one of his friends, the one nicknamed Sampson because of his amazing strength, tried to inhabit, but fell and was carried away by the silent treacherous waters to the waterfall that finished the job. His terrified screams echoing above the fast-moving waters of the waterfall, crashing against the jagged rocks in the seemingly harmless frothy pool below.

Pa Joe Joe bends over, his hands on his trembling knees, begins choking on his ragged breath. He looks up at the unoccupied seat in the cleft of the rock. It seems to be beckoning him, even coaxing him to come sit on it as he used to. The night creatures too, are anxiously awaiting the master of the forest to take his seat, before they come out to frolic at his feet. Cavorting for his pleasure.

Pa Joe Joe straightens up, his arms hugging his chest and faces his now nemesis, the rock. Now mocking him, daring him to come sit in its cleft. To once again climb way above the rock, up it's dangerous and jagged slopes, as he had done conquering it, all those many years ago...

From this vantage position on the ground, he keeps looking up at the rock that for the first time seems to be reaching way pass the clouds, straight into the heavens. He looks at the smaller spear like rocks, at the boulders, that seemed to be sitting perilously on ledges below his rock. Now, they all seem threatening and insurmountable as if protecting 'his rock' and it's cleft – where he would often sit becoming one with the deafening waterfall as it emptied itself in the pool below.

It's mighty roars never interrupting his thoughts nor intruding into his dreams of one day bringing fame and fortune to this, his small unspoilt village – to build that little cottage, that's what the Irish couple called their little house high up on the hill. Only his was to be built near the stream in the middle of the forest, where he would take his Josephine after making her his wife. There she would sing to him and the babies they would have, anytime she wanted. No need for her to go to America to have a singing career!

The cackling from above, draws Pa Joe Joe's gaze to the never before seen flock of blackbirds that have suddenly taken over his cleft. He smiles cynically: *Might as well*, he thinks looking at the birds. He brings his hands to his waist, twisting from side to side. His soft flesh offering no resistance – he promises himself to do something about that, to toughen up. He tries surveying what he could see of his old haunt, the forest, but there isn't much to see with the encroaching darkness – not even with the night lights of hundreds maybe thousands of *'candle flies'*, that would suffice much younger eyes. No, the light isn't enough for his older eyes to see by now.

He heaves his shoulders, is that in defeat? Is it that many years since his body and mind defeated and conquered anything or anyone when challenged? Pa Joe Joe steels himself, he has to admit that he is no longer *the* Joseph Celestine and, *she* no longer was his Josephine – *'the old woman had seen to that'*. **"Now sing aloud Josephine, you are in New York – the world is your stage, yours and the old woman's."** His mercurial words tinged with pain and regret, reverberates all around the forest frightening the nightlife that has come out to lay at his feet or stand at attention paying homage to him. Now they should stop all this – can they not see that he no longer has dominion over them, that he no longer is the master of the forest? Now he's just another washed up wannabe who only made it as a preacher man! Yes, the old woman whom he hates has won. Damn it! Now sing! Sing! Sing Josephine! He keeps shouting out until his hoarseness and tiredness brings him to his knees.

Chapter 9

Ma Jo Jo just won't quit with her reminiscing but this time she does not delve in the distant past, just two weeks ago … Ma Jo Jo's eyes the flowers in the gleaming brass pots and snorts; She does not want to admit it, but they are beautiful. She is annoyed that they are not from the village but from some fancy flower shop in **quiteo quiteo**, a place from **where ever**, very far away. These flowers were purchased by Mother Gloria who has a reputation of trying to outdo everyone. Ma Jo Jo steups and turns away from the much-admired gleaming brass pots and their beautiful flowers, wondering aloud what was wrong with the customary used flowers and plants of the village.

Why couldn't they sit just as grandly in that large gleaming pot and the smaller ones around the room. The hibiscus, Ixora's, hydrangeas and especially the wonderfully hued and speckled leaves of the croton plants of which more could be used and freely too! Not one villager would have minded if Mother Gloria broke off branches, leaves, or bunches of flowers from their shrubs – anything for their revered Pa Joe Joe. *"Changes coming to dis village, wedda alyuh like it or not"*, the aristocratic leaning head of the village council would state emphatically to anyone who would question her for implementing a new rule or change. Ma Jo Jo Looks across to the slim and Pretty Woman fussing at her husband's bed; She was quite assertive too. Ma Jo Jo shrugs her shoulders – she does not care anymore, in fact she had stopped caring even about the whispers that the church helpers shared; That, *'Mother Gloria was now in Pa Joe Joe's life'*. She shrugged those rumors away, knowing the awful things, the lies that have been **spread** about her so many years ago; her involvement with Mr. Leo.

Looking around the room, she has to admit that the artistically arranged flowers, does brighten up the otherwise drab room; save for the crisp white sheet that overlaid the equally crisp white beautifully embroidered linen bedspread, on which her husband now lie. This beautiful unexpected gift was from the Older One, on a return visit for Ma Z's eightieth birthday. The bedspread was used on *special* occasions like Christmas and Easter, though no one ever had the privilege of lying on it. This now, is such an occasion; The dying body of her husband, Pa Joe Joe deserves to be laid on this, a bedspread this eye-catching.

Ma Jo Jo gets no satisfaction from the admiring or envious stares that the bedspread elicits from the women who have come to offer words of support or encouragement to her.

From her seat across the room, she feels a rush of sadness as she looks upon the prematurely aged man lying there on the bed. She feels saddened by her **weakness**, for that what it clearly was, **weakness**, in her acquiescing to the old woman's wishes, that she leave him to pursue a singing career in New York which led to their tumultuous life and now to this, it's end. Sadness for the villagers who believed that they were denied the chance of being placed high up on the so called 'map' by his incarceration. Ma Jo Jo, the tears distorting her view, is hoping that the wonderful memories of their early years were flowing through the mind in the nearly wasted body, that of Joseph Celestine lying on the bed.

She is reduced to a crumpled mess now. She is seeing the blood and the body of the older and drunk man that was severely kicked off hers, as they laid intertwined between the tall grass and bushes. Her Joseph, his terror filled eyes not meeting hers, looking away in hopelessness, disbelief. Then running away in his blood splattered clothing. Blood dripping from the terrible wounds on his left hand, the hand which held the weapon with which he had just done the dastardly act.

Ma Jo Jo let's lose with one of her signature sighs, only this one is fraught with regret. Thankfully, the foot traffic through the bedroom and hallway, leading to the church outback is experiencing a welcomed lull. She hugs herself, closes her eyes and begins to viciously rockaway – the chair groaning and squealing under her weight. Now, she's unleashing the spigot of tears that won't wash away the memory of that last fiasco on the stage ...

He's there, way in the back of the room, slumped shoulders, hat deep on his head, head hung low as he is slipping out of the room. Yes, she had chosen her career over him, and in so doing, sealed their faith, destroyed their lives that very day ...

Abruptly, Ma Jo Jo has turned off the spigot of tears. She's listening to the labored breathing coming from the bed across the room, just under the window. She hears the quickening footsteps coming in from the drawing room; someone else has heard the labored breathing too. Ma Jo Jo quickly closes her eyes, she knows to whom those footsteps belong. It's *'that'* Mother Gloria whom she understands but does not like one bit, even though she knows that the Pretty Woman was given a bad 'rep' by those insecure women who kept their wary eyes on her, whenever around their men. The truly highly principled woman first grew a *'don't care a damn'* attitude and did or said absolutely nothing to allay the village women fear of her. The *country boukies* she would sniff disdainfully whenever she was made aware of *their bad talking her*. Was it any surprise that it was rumored that she was one of Pa Joe Joe's *'Sweet Ting'* his *'Outside 'Oman'*. This untrue rumor did not deter or perturb her, she just went on doing her work for the principled and godly man.

The rumors of Pa Joe Joe's dalliances with the women in an out of his church did not sully or destroy his reputation, though the untrue rumors did destroy some of those unfortunate women's – nothing could stick on *'their boy'*. Everyone remembers his athletic prowess; and only that he was robbed of the opportunity to keep putting the village on the international stage. He having been derailed by the young Josephine, the Jezebel! Yes, nothing could stop*, 'dey boy'* and after his being *'away'* for the five years, he had become one of the country's best medicine men /faith healers. This was proven by the large number of **outsiders** coming into the village before *'foreday'* **mornings**, three days per week.

Yes, even before the dawning of those days, the people would occupy every seat available in the church. The 'overflow', not minding having to sit outside under the mango and coconut trees on makeshift benches. Even Ma Jo Jo's stone bleach sat grateful *behinds*, happy to have gotten a seat, any seat. The outsiders having to leave their homes, **early O clock** in order to be one of the lucky ones to see Pa Joe Joe that day.

These people depended on the part time vendors who would absent themselves from their work in the estates. Some of their children would go to school, **half day**, the latter half of the school day because of their parent's reliance on them to help with the preparation of the meals which the *'outsiders'* feasted on. Most of the outsiders doubling up on their lunch orders to take back to their loved ones, since most of the delicious meals, they had never eaten or not had in a long time.

The villagers on the whole, even those who halfheartedly dabbled with the local handicraft in expectancy of sales from the outsider's, were thankful for the extra finances that blessed their wallets and pockets. *'The Old Timers'* steadfastly holding onto the belief that Pa Joe Joe was someone special, most not sure if they should use the word a savior, not wanting to be blasphemous, settle for a *benefactor*. They were certain that their showers of blessings were because of him, his goodness. The little matter of him being, if it was even possible, a **village ram**, *a wildman*, a *lothario* it was no concern of theirs. *'They would not sit upon the river stone and talk de river bad!' Definitely don't bite the hand that feeds them.*

~~~

Through her narrowed eyes, Ma Jo Jo, still pretending to be asleep, looks on as Mother Gloria straddles the doorway; One of her hands on her almost girlish hips, the other waving in the air, summoning to her, Elvin and his friends who are lying under the mango tree.

Ma Jo Jo listens to her commanding or rather ordering the young men under her breath. Then in what seems to be a matter of seconds, the bed with her husband on it, is lifted and carried to the opposite side of the room, just under the window. The curtain is drawn apart and the natural light comes filtering through the branches and leaves of the great big calabash mango tree and onto his face.
~~~

The gentle breeze that is now allowed into the room, easily pervades each and every flower filled brass pot – gently, ever so gently, whispering to the closed petals urging them to explode their pot pouri of scents throughout the little house.

Awkwardly, Mother Gloria reaches across the bed to gather the free-flowing nylon curtain that has begun to play with and teased the immobile Pa Joe Joe's upper body; Her breast brushing against his face in the process. She quickly glances across at Ma Jo Jo, and at the same time feels a surge of anger arising from deep within. Why was she feeling this angry, was she beginning to let those ugly rumors that was spread throughout the years get to her now? Mother Gloria again looks to Ma Jo Jo – the alternative of her not having her breasts touch her husband's face as she stretches across the bed, was her climbing on top and crumbling the lily-white linen bedding which came from New York and thus causing Ma Jo Jo to have a stroke or heart attack. Mother Gloria exaggerates to herself, while choking on her giggles.

Mother Gloria flashes a cynical grin over at Ma Jo Jo – she has seen her blinking eyelids. Ma Jo Jo still pretending to be asleep does not return a smile or a grin, so Mother Gloria sends her a deathly 'cuteye' as she leaves the room. This too, Ma Jo Jo ignores, feeling *'cock sure'* that Pa Joe Joe is still aware of everything that's going on around him, so she decides to stay on the 'high road', be circumspect. Instead, she affixes her eyes on the beautiful bedding – The gift from the Older One. The Older One, Ma Jo Jo repeats the nickname she detests, knowing that the women in the neighborhood had affixed on the misunderstood child. Branding her as being rude and disrespectful, her needing a *'good cuttail'*, a sound beating and this was only because she would persist on explaining herself when accused of wrongdoing, even though she was being shouted down too shut her *'trap'*, shut her *'beak'* right now – stop talking! With much derision Ma Jo Jo slowly plays on the detestable name once again, *'Older One'*, then goes off into a fitful sleep.

Chapter 10

With her face pressed against one of the board windows in her drawing room, Ma Jo Jo marvels at the kaleidoscope of colors laying before her, they representing every fruit and fallen vegetable that floated in from the neighborhood yards, higher up the hill and even from her yard too. As if to give credence to what she is thinking, a branch from the lone 'Mammy Apple' tree in her yard comes crashing down and with it, the lone first ever fruit from the tree. Ma Jo Jo wants to run outside in the *'pelting rain'* to gather the busted fruit but can only watch in dismay as the gushing water takes it farther downhill.

A *male* tree, everyone thought of the tree that never bore a single fruit for all the years it stood in Ma Jo Jo's yard. Trees of this type which are found in mountainous regions, were thought of as fakes to have grown out of their natural environment.

Now the rain beating furiously at and seeping through the cracks of the board window is forcing Ma Jo Jo to back away but not before she takes in what little she could see of her neighborhood, that is being blanketed in blackness. The silhouettes of the nearby little wooden houses, the rains rushing off their tin roofs, make them seem like river boats run aground.

~~~

Ma Jo Jo bites into her trembling lips; She admonishes herself for the tears; She's fed up with the tears. She had even promised her husband that she'll shed no tears for him – he had made that request of her; She didn't question it. Ma Jo Jo sharply pulls herself up, what
~~~

did she say, her husband? Yes, *her husband* dammit, he was Hers! Hers! Hers!

Now and mercifully so, she gives into the throbbing pain in her knees, slumps down on the floor, is swallowed up by the mass of colors in the rug and comes face to face once again with the dying or by now, dead bird.

Ma Jo Jo's thoughts are up and running, thoughts of her past, her yesterdays...The last time Pa Joe Joe *really* touched her ...It was soon after his release from prison. He was sitting at the side of the bed; His strong lean fingers playing with the small of her back, pressing into it, her flesh, her soul ...

Ma Jo Jo dare not open her eyes, she can sense him fumbling. Mo Jo Jo knows exactly what it's all about, even before the belt buckle hits the floor. She flips over, hungrily, greedily, reaching up to Pa Joe Joe, her husband. No! She is reaching out to Joseph Celestine, they are reaching out to each other as should have been done, all through those lost years.

Ma Jo Jo sees the gaily printed drape that separates the living room from the bedroom as it begins to sway in the windless house. Ma Jo Jo sees the little fingers holding onto the fabric, gathering it together in her little hands and from the bottom of the drape she sees the painted tiny toenails still fresh and bright with the red cutex nail polish, the only brand and color available from the Chineseman's shop. Ma Jo Jo had painted and kissed every one of those tiny toes on drying – kissing and counting, causing the little girl to giggle and laugh hysterically.

Ma Jo Jo is beginning to be caught up in a vicious whirlwind, the entangling bushes, the courthouse, and Joseph Celestine recoiling from her in horror ...Ma Jo Jo is trying to fight her way out of the whirlwind ...

He abruptly gets up from the bed. Now, she is seeing the hate in his eyes. He is no longer her Joseph Celestine, Pa Joe Joe has taken his place. She is seeing the overriding frustration mixed in with heartache and pain – total confusion!

The Older One is still clutching the drape in her hand as he storm's past her. She has heard not one word from Pa Joe Joe's tightly sealed lips, but her words, her heartbreaking question keeps on ringing in Ma Jo Jo's ears; *"Why he doh like meh? Why he ent like meh?"* Knowing that she could never give the little girl an answer, and with her heartbreaking question ringing in her ears, Ma Jo Jo holds her tightly in her arms, the child's unanswerable question, of why doesn't he like me, squeezing her heart like a vice.

~~~

Ma Jo Jo, a determined glint in her eyes, gets up from the rug, having seen the very last flutter of the bird's wings and the partial closure of its glazed eyes and she promises "As soon as the storm passes I'm going to give you a beautiful burial, right under that great big mossy branch that I often see you on. A funeral just like the one the village gave to Pa Joe Joe." Then, as an afterthought says steely, "like *I* gave to him."

Once again in her bedroom and seated on her rocking chair, Ma Jo Jo's thoughts are about the days leading up to Pa Joe Joe's death. Luckily for her, who knew nothing about the customs concerning Pa Joe Joe's religion and burial. There were available to her *"Leaders"*, the two strangers who took up residence in the church out back, to whom the villagers flocked to get answers. The one thing that seemed to irk Ma Jo Jo, was the way they wore their self-import on their sleeves, leaving many in the village to compare them with their beloved Pa Joe Joe and they, coming way up short. They stuck to themselves and in the church until the mid-morning sun beating down unmercifully on the tin roof would force them out, only to take the seats under the shady mango tree, which Elvin and his friends readily vacated.

With all that was going on, Pa Joe Joe was still *'here'* taking everything in. He was slyly looking at Ma Jo Jo with death filled eyes and she doing likewise – looking at him. He felt her even when she would slip away to consult with the two men, his keepers for the time being but soon to be sidelined by his friend, the high priest from the mountain, who would definitely be showing these *'show boats'*, how things are done!
~~~

Pa Joe Joe hears the slow and steady thumping of the drums. He frowns deeply; This is not how it is supposed to be, what are they all about? He begins to get restless, lying there on the bed – his spirit does, since his body, any part of it had long past the stage of moving on its own. Hence the presence of those two men in his church.

Now, were they, the drummers, trying to send his stubborn spirit home? That would be highly unusual since he was neither in pain or 'ready', his mind, that is. As for his spirit he thought that it had to await *that one*. He knows that he was in for the battle of his life with *him*. He often refusing to give him the respect that he craved and the comparisons that he wanted with the truly *Great One*, whose path Pa Joe Joe, now regrets not always following.

Pa Joe Joe sighs with relief on the understanding that the drummers he was hearing, were not at all about him but were practicing down by the river for a competition that they had entered, and were now highly favored to win, having been placed in the semifinals. Before entering the competition, they had even discussed their participation with him and seeked his advice, he having a broad and wide ranging knowledge of things cultural.

Pa Joe Joe is hearing the putt, putt, putt, of the motorbike, he sighs blissfully and hopes that the peaceful glow spreading across his soul, would manifest itself on his face when she comes in to see him. The Young One has arrived on the puttering motorbike of the boy from the city and would soon be inside sitting at his bedside. Momentarily, he wandered at the status of their relationship. For her sake, he has decided to put on a bright face, if that is at all possible, not to let the darkness that has clouded most of his life, to completely take over the end of it now.

Again, for her sake, he would go out as they say, with a celebratory loud bang! He had stood at the sidelines watching her transform from a bud to a beautiful rose, had seen the blush of the first petal as it hesitantly unfurled; then each one thereafter, strong, fragile, innocent, bold! Yes, he was always there at the sidelines too least she stumbled as she was apt to do.

He did not let her see the tears when she offered him the award won for her play, at just twenty years of age. Stoically, he stood there in the church and turned her away. He knew just what she was trying to do, but she could not make amends for the disaster the **Older One** had brought to his promising life. He remembers the rush of emotions that had embroiled him then; The love, pity, the forced misplaced anger that was smoldering all these years, came rushing to the forefront. This was not fair, she was not Ma Jo Jo who destroyed them both by seeking her singing career, nor was she the resultant **Older One**!

At his rejection, the Young One dissolved in tears on the floor in the middle of the church. Why was she doing this to him, cloaking him in an ironclad sheet of guilt? The night was hers to celebrate, to bask in her award-winning victory with her friends, enjoying the glow of the city lights – not sit on the dusty floor of his village church, trying to guilt him into loving her with her award! Damn it! He loved her already didn't she know that, didn't the whole village?

The Young One collected herself and picked up her award which he had refused. She turned to him, fresh tears rolling down her already tear stained cheeks, once more offering her **bribe**, her love through the trophy. Her actions begging him to love her, pleading that she should not be a reminder of his past, his unfilled life, of what could have been. Pa Joe Joe began seeing the images of the **Older One** through her – he steeled himself and slowly walked away from the **Younger One**, who in turn fled through the church's door.

Pa Joe Joe heard the choked sobs coming from the doorway that gives easy access from the house to the church and used mostly at night-time. It was Ma Jo Jo, clutching at her chest, her eyes imploring him to show the child the immense love that he has and hides from her. Pa Joe Joe shot her a contemptuous look before she backed away behind the curtain, letting it fall back in place where it belonged – in essence blocking out what never could be. Pa Joe Joe drew a deep sigh, stuck his pipe into his mouth, sucking angrily on it. He had seen the back of the Young One as she fled through the church's door. She was filled with rage and hate, filled with murderous thoughts, all directed to the woman who had interrupted her life once again – the Older One.

But for a moment, Pa Joe Joe worried over her. He knew exactly where she was going – she, running through the darkened tracks to the river. He was sure that the candle flies, those hundreds of fireflies would light her way and the maddening night noises of the '*Cigals*' and other night insects and animals would lead her there, where her affinity with the river would calm and heal her. Pa Joe Joe was sure that '*he too*', would be there, somewhere in the bushes, his protective eyes watching over her.

Eventually, Pa Joe Joe redirected his anger and concern on himself, his **jing toe**, his busted big toe, that seem not to be healing, despite the medicines that he himself had administered both internally and externally. The toe seeming to be getting on the darker side of purple. Pa Joe Joe smiled sardonically and noted that the maxim '*man heal thyself*', sure wasn't applicable to him and his busted toe.

Pa Joe Joe looked around his darkened church and felt a sense of helplessness; Mother Grace and Miss Boney were due back from one of the islands in two days. They were on one of their monthly jaunts, purchasing the oils, powders, herbs and spices needed for making his medicines and bath potions, that were seldom had in the surrounding villages and towns, or if available, were never in enough quantity to satisfy his large and ever growing clientele. Or would be way too exorbitantly priced; that his pricing would be way above the little man's pay grade, his pocket. The next best, but never seriously considered solution, would be him **stretching** his powders by mixing in something less expensive or watering down his potions – something that he would never do.

~~~

Lying here in his fevered state and slyly watching her, he again began to ruminate on his life, Ma Jo Jo and his. They had been then and even now, dancing their crafty and complicated dance all these years. Movement sensual, full of love of hate, never touching, yet full of feelings – keeping their respective distance.

Even now, with death clouding his vision, he is still slyly watching her, just as she too, him. Watching his fanciful and artful
~~~

footwork, his deceitful attempted embraces. Ma Jo Jo is matching his flourishes, going toe to toe with him – never to be outdone after all these years.

Pa Joe Joe feels his rapid breaths beginning to choke him. Could feel her cold breath or is it death's, on his chest? How dare she dance this close to him now? Surely, she should know that she is cheating – won't be the first time he thinks darkly.

Is her brightly colored garbs a part of the dance too, a nod to her anticipated victory? Is she trying to tell him something, maybe that death is close by, that she has won the dance off – that the victory waited on close to forty years is finally coming her way, the old woman's and the other in New York?

What is she doing, what is he really seeing, is he hallucinating? Ma Jo Jo, she is furiously twirling and twisting. The fabric of her skirt, swishing and swooshing – lashing at him with her every movement, that he has to quickly dance out of her way, never missing a beat or step though. Her bulging eyes and blood red lips, grotesque looking, even frightening. Her bright multi-colored skirt, its colors leaping out at him, quite a contrast to the soberly clad people seated outside in the cool night, or those respectfully filing past his bed, the not yet dead man.

Subconsciously, Pa Joe Joe begins to twitch as he again hears the resumption of the soft tapping of the drums. The drummers having taken a break, to *'jort'* down on the just cooked wild meat and ground provisions, the delicious scents having tantalized their taste buds for a while now.

Pa Joe Joe is becoming agitated and perplexed once more. Why were they turning their sacred tradition on its head? He is still here! Why won't they stop this drumming! His body begins to twitch violently in protest. Then the little voice in his head reminds him that the drumming was coming from the **youthmen** down by the river. They are participating in the competition, **remember**? It questions, Pa Joe Joe sighs. Ma Jo Jo too, was not doing a victory dance over him, her skirt was not swishing nor swooshing, its fabric brushing against his face in triumph over him, this immobile man.

He hears her whispering encouraging words as she gently shows those lingering mourners out of the now hot and cramped room. Those people who have come to pay their respects – paying homage to him, the spiritual leader whom the many from time to time seeked out and trusted to cure them of whatever ailed them.

If he wasn't already close to the end of his journey, to the **next plain**, he would have indulged in one last chuckle as he hears the shuffling feet which alerted him that *'they'* were in the room once again and if his fevered brain has it right, he surmises that this might be their umpeenth time.

In the quiet of his room, Pa Joe Joe listens intently to the heavy breathing; this confirms that they are indeed in his room, his keepers. The two previously **maga, maga**, preachers – their once skinny frames now so large that their gaits had become a series of shuffling and mincing steps.

These two men, from another village, since becoming preachers, *'fakes'* to a lot of the people; They have been gorging themselves on every and any appetizing dish, brought to them by their grateful clientele. Pa Joe Joe clearly hears the two men at his bedside hmming and hawing. He imagines that they are **down** in his face, searching; maybe seeking for signs of when his stubborn spirit would take leave? Though his sense of hearing is leaving him, just as his vision is doing too, he also knows when they are shuffling away, as he feels the rush of cold air as they open and close the door on exiting the room.

He knows too, that someone, maybe Mother Gloria had covered his body with what has to be one of Ma Jo Jo's lily-white sheets, which she only uses on special occasions. Guess his upcoming death is a special occasion, he thinks wryly. Lying on his deathbed, he smiles at the irony of his busted toe taking him out. He, who treated and cured what many of the fancy doctors in the city and towns could not. Now, not even the toe being amputated could save him – he had not taken care of it. He was suffering from **blood poison**, sepsis and it is now too late. Ironically, he is being felled by a mere busted toe, his big toe!

Pa Joe Joe lying there on his bed, feels the sudden silence that has pervaded the once chattering crowd outside. Then, on hearing the wild cheers and effusive congratulations, he momentarily musters the smile that was waiting to burst forth from within his heart, to manifest itself on his face. She really did arrive! It is really her on the putt! Putt! Putt! Motorcycle.

Pa Joe Joe was concerned that after the fiasco in his church, that they would never speak again, what with her subsequent moving out of the village and her infrequent visits back to the old woman on the hill.

Pa Joe Joe sighs, happily so. The past had thrown up many steep walls that were insurmountable for even him, too many roadblocks that made it impossible to navigate his way to her, but surely, she the Young One, should know how he loved her so. Why was he now being racked with guilt and worry?

The crowd outside was giving her *'pips'* for yet another successful play that the majority would never see – they not leaving the village to go into the city. It was alright, every one of them had heard about her success through word of mouth or read the reviews in a newspaper that were brought in at night by those who worked outside the village and passed around to whoever wanted *'a'* read. The Chineseman, only selling one newspaper for the week – the widely read and popular Sunday newspaper. Both, the younger and older men needing their weekend fix of the comics, especially with the exploits of Dick Tracy, Mandrake and the Phantom – ditto the women and their fixation with Dr. Morgan and his nurse June.

Pa Joe Joe smiles nostalgically knowing that the Younger One had become the villages latest version of the *'Great White Hope'*. They won't give up, won't they? They, praying that she would scale the tallest greasy pole, make the highest jumps, step back and watch satisfactorily as she let loose the slim bamboo pole in her hand as it quivers through the air, finally embedding itself in the ground, farther, much farther than any of her competitors.

Pa Joe Joe feels the tears trickling down his cheeks, he knows that those thoughts of her athletic exploits were all about him and his youthful days on the tracks and fields and what could have been – that he was delving way back into the forbidden past.

Pa Joe Joe knows that she is now in the room, not only because of the cool air that comes in as she opens the door – he smells her too, cinnamon, nutmeg, vanilla; **lilac** she would often correct him, with eye roles in exasperation. She having to continuously correct him on her latter scent. He didn't care, he only knew that as a young girl she would smell of the cakes and other goodies, that she would help the old woman, a vendor, bake in her clay oven out back in her shed on weekends. Then, with other competing vendors, sell outside the school or bus stop; Wherever there was a mass of people.

Pa Joe Joe tries willing his face to the direction of the scent and at the same time tries to blink away the veil of death which is quickly covering his failing eyes. But for a moment, he sees the beautiful face with the wistful smile looking down on him. Then, in a flash the face and smile is gone from his clouded vision. Thankfully he is left with the scent – the sweet scent of her.

She looks at the trembling figure trying to rise towards her and grasps at the feeble hand reaching out to her. She places it between hers, squeezing it gently, yet worrying if she is hurting him. She kneels at the side of his bed, his *bony* hand still in hers. Uncomfortably reaching across, she rests his hand on her cheek hoping that he could receive the love she is furiously sending his way. Quickly she lets the hand slip away and repositions herself, cradling his head in her hands.

"Don't be sad for me, it's okay, I'll be alright little one", he manages, his voice a mere whisper as he feels her tears falling on his face. Pa Joe Joe, Ma Jo Jo's husband keeps peering towards the little one, since what his diminishing eyes would allow – is only her silhouette. Her tears keep coming – Pa Joe Joe knows that he has to do something or say anything, to help her, even if it kills him. He is going anyway, he thinks. "Aie, stop it **cakes,** stop it right now!" He can imagine her wincing at yet another of his corny nicknames, the one she hated the most as a child and he has dredged up for the last time.

The silhouette is now gone and there is so much to be said to her. He wants to let her know how proud that this, latest play, is heading to New York. He wants to share that he too Joseph

Celestine, was once headed abroad but to the U.K, to put their country, their little village on the world stage, but she already knew that, didn't she? The older heads talking ad-nauseam about that and also what stopped him.

Pa Joe Joe is becoming restless and agitated – this is not how he wants his end to be. He wants her to know that Ma Jo Jo had shared that the play; she had dedicated it to him, but he knew that *'it'*, was all about him, wasn't it? The words that Pa Joe Joe begins to speak, he knows is all in his head and would not be manifested out of his mouth to her. '**Hey cakes, the play ends like this, doesn't it, you let me die didn't you?'** Pa Joe Joe pauses, then continues, sharing easily; **I've got to go cakes, the spirits are coming for me, I can feel them – the Great God in the sky has summoned me, do you think that I did right by him. In the play, did he himself come to take me away, did you bestow that great honor on me cakes?**

The Young One feels his head slipping out of her hands as he tries in vain to turn his head in the direction where he last heard her voice. He, now being unable to see anything. Even the scent of her is fast fading; His precious cakes.

Pa Joe Joe's eyes begin to flutter wildly. This is all Ma Jo Jo's fault! She had facilitated the Older and Younger One's move to the old woman's on the hill – they looking down on him. Was she, the old woman, taunting him, punishing him maybe? He would show her, ignore them both! But he was fooling no one but himself. He had fallen in love with the Young One the moment that he saw her in Ma Jo Jo's hands after her birth.

...Pa Joe Joe is hearing the precocious little thing's girlish laughter ringing in his ears, as she played at **ring a ring a roses** and **brown girl in the ring**, a game for more than two, but all the same, enjoyed by the Young One, as she giggled and squealed, continuously hugging and kissing *'her partner,'* Ma Jo Jo, who would often feign being tired, to bring the game to a conclusion. How could he not fall in love with her? The laughter full off gay abandon, was long gone, chased away by him, his pretense of not loving her – his refusal to move on from the ugly past.

Pa Joe Joe begins to breathe rapidly – is she still here? **Aye Gramps!** He would do anything to hear her mischievously call out to him by that name; That once made him cringe, as she ran pass in front of his church on her way to the river. He was surprised the first time he was called by the name, that the axe he was wielding, stayed suspended in the air for a while before it finally met with the log he was chopping.

He had thrown his head back, laughing heartily. Then he heard Ma Jo Jo snickering behind the drape over the doorway. He looked up angrily, just in time to see her sneaking away. It was all her fault! Her fault too! Pa Joe Joe's feverish brain kept thinking of the old woman on the hill, whose name he had vowed never to speak. The woman who had taken away the forty or so years, that he and Ma Jo Jo could of had, no, should of had!

She had taken them away by living her life through her daughter Josephine, through the melodious voice of his **Josephine**. Her once craved life for the stage, the popping lights of the cameras had eluded her because that life was unavailable, was unheard of for any one of the villagers, at that time. So, she became obsessed, even determined that Josephine succeeded in living that life for her.

Pa Joe Joe again tries to steer his thoughts to the Young One, his **Cakes**. With his twisted and confused mind going every which way. Pa Joe Joe begins to think about the *other one* whom he seemed to obey more often than not. He knows that he doesn't have the power to let him watch over and protect his **Cakes**, in what was sure to be his miserable and wasteful afterlife. Pa Joe Joe sighs regretfully, knowing that, *'that one'* never had and would never have that power.

He had obeyed him by never giving Ma Jo Jo a chance of what was once a hope for beautiful life, no matter how much it pained him for holding back – no matter how much he ached for her and how much he regretted not obeying the one and only true one, **THE GREAT ONE!**

Pa Joe Joe hears the bells and whistles, the banging of the drums – he is now in complete darkness. The icy cold wind is coming in, in a rush. Something akin to a sudden storm is brewing, kicking up dust clouds, rooting up the dry and barren trees and angrily hurling stones and boulders at unseen targets. An unbearable heat begins to envelop him. Then the cold, the heat, the heat, the cold, then back to the heat. Oh! Suddenly it dawns on Pa Joe Joe that to whom he had given much leeway in his life, often stepping off the straight and narrow path was ready for him!

Through the darkness he sees them come creeping in, why are they doing this so stealthily? He understands the darkness, that's how they operate, covering their victims in total darkness in order to steal and plunder their minds and souls. Afraid that the light might hinder their creeping into the lives of those whom their master had chosen for destruction though with the supposed victim tacit approval.

Puzzled, Pa Joe Joe looks at the way they are coming in; Still creeping into his life at this stage. He was a preacher, he chose the darkness, he disobeyed **'The Great One'**. Even with the brightest of lights shining down on him, lighting his path, yes, he chose to stumble over the rocks and boulders into the darkness in which he might now regretfully live in for eternity!

Pa Joe Joe sighs on seeing *the men who were sent*, nervously looking around the room. Yes, it was him! Pa Joe Joe was sure that *'he'* had sent them ahead of him, to check out his adversary. *'He'*, expecting a colossal battle from Pa Joe Joe but he was wrong. Pa Joe Joe is ready – regretfully, he acknowledges that he had already given himself up to him, through the hatred that he harbored in his heart for the old woman on the hill and his never being able to free himself from his willful self-imprisonment, by not giving to Ma Jo Jo the love she deserved – that he kept locked in his heart. Pa Joe Joe had tangled many times before with *'him'*, had long arduous battles, winning many but **only** when he sought out and had the **Great One** on his side.

Once, Pa Joe Joe was tall, strong, big muscled and most handsome too. *That One* did not like this one bit, he thought of himself the strongest and handsomest creature on all the earth. Oftentimes, with a finger tapping his strong chin, he would even shoot an inquiring eye toward the heavens – he the vain one! Dare he go there, challenging the master?

He comes in and gives Pa Joe Joe a look so frighteningly sinister, that even Pa Joe Joe is taken aback. Now, he places his grotesquely deformed hands on his face. The long claw like fingers splayed over his deceitful face, the equally long and dirty fingernails buried in his long greasy looking hair. Gleefully, he looks down at his prize, Pa Joe Joe, whom he thinks that he had snatched from right under the nose of the **GREAT ONE**. He keeps looking at Pa Joe Joe lying helplessly on the bed and shakes his head, yes! Then he quickly looks up to the heavens and his head falls sharply onto his chest shaking from side to side, the gesture saying, no!

Slowly, very slowly, he slinks away alone. Is this in defeat? Bright glowing orange flames of fire begins spitting out from the hole in his face – he is no longer the handsome one he thinks of himself. He is alone, his disciples long gone even before his arrival, they, not wanting to be around, knowing his fury when handed a defeat and this one with Pa Joe Joe is a major one.

But wait, he did deliberately choose this preacher man. He led him to destroy those people's chances of happiness all those years ago. He caused them intolerable grief! He committed intolerable sins! How was he forgiven, the sneaky bastard, did he repent, asked for forgiveness even now on his deathbed?

He looks up angrily at the heavens knowing that's what has happened! Pa Joe Joe asked for and was forgiven his sins, even now on his deathbed! Being the crafty devil, he is and not one to give up easily, he sneakily turns around and creeps back in. Once again, standing over Pa Joe Joe, looking down at him lying there, he begins swaying from side to side, his chain around his waist, going all the way down to the floor, making unmelodious noises. A rope circling over his head in lasso like fashion, as if readying to rope Pa Joe Joe in, cattle like style, if he should attempt to run away.

He bends even lower, quizzically searching, searching Pa Joe Joe's face. Even in his dying state Pa Joe Joe feels nauseated, maybe from the unbearable stench and unbearable heat emanating from the hole in the face over him. Waves of revulsion begins washing over Pa Joe Joe for what he has perhaps done to himself. He just could not let go of his lost five years.

The deceitful one's face is now just mere inches from Pa Joe Joe's, his nose nearly touching his. His neck swiveling from cheek to cheek, very close to his open mouth. Hoping to catch a faint breath of life coming from his failing lungs? It is indeed a comical sight to see, he wanting to ensure victory over this doomed man before taking his leave.

Finally convinced that Pa Joe Joe is soon to be no more, that he has truly lost him to the **One Above**, he snorts and spits at him. That angry red sparks, black smoke and soot rushing out of the hole in his face, covers the bed of the near dead man. Clearly angry, the deceitful one, snorts again, stomps his feet and shakes his fists at the heavens above. He will not easily get over this one, Pa Joe Joe. He clearly is not satisfied with his performance. He had taken away his dreams of athletic fame, the woman of his dreams, crushed the spirit and hopes of the village, sent him away for five years and what did he, the deceitful one get in return? A healer, an uplifter, *a do gooder*!

The deceitful one looks up at the heavens – *'He'* had forgiven Pa Joe Joe his shortcomings, didn't **He**? Pa Joe Joe also was thought to be the victim, wasn't he? Not fair! He snorts again, stomping his feet like a defiant child. He looks up once again, intending to shake his fists at the *'victor'* up there but shakes his head instead. His long dirty hair falling over, covering his face. He isn't sure just how far he could go.

He again looks around for his disciples and sees that they had long gotten lost, vamoosed, taken their leave knowing that he would be on the war path, his spiteful best for being vanquished for the final time, through this formidable foe, the preacher man.

He looks at Pa Joe Joe, scornfully so, this time. He had so much plans for him, whenever his end came. He was supposed to be his right-hand man, his chief architect. Angrily, he lowers his rope and with the chain dragging behind him, he skulks away, still spitting fire and smoke at the thought of Pa Joe Joe.

Time after time Pa Joe Joe had disappointed him, what with him healing and casting out the demons that he had sent into his would-be acolytes. Surely, Pa Joe Joe would have known that it was he, who sent in the demons into those wretched souls, not only to torture them at his pleasure, that they be at his mercy but to show the *'One Above'* that he was still relevant.

Still, if the **One Above** releases Pa Joe Joe to him, he would punish him and severely so. He who thought that he could serve two masters at the same time; he would have him groan and beg for another chance to serve him, but faithfully so this time! Then, yes then, he would bring him down lower than the lowest of his disciples!

The deceitful one stops dead in his tracks. The chain dragging behind him, making the most horrendous of noises and then deathly silence as it comes to a sudden stop. His eyebrows arched with a nonverbal question. He puts a twisted finger to his mouth, gnawing on its gnarled nail. He quickly pivots around as if hoping to catch Pa Joe Joe standing, or dancing a jig, perhaps? Oh! He thought that he had seen a pithy smile on the supposedly dead man's face. Filled with rage, he swears that if his request was ever granted to get Pa Joe Joe's soul, he would deal with him most forcefully whenever they meet in the pits of hell!

Not one to give up easily, an afterthought comes to him – his deserved punishment. Pa Joe Joe had made the **ONE ABOVE** victorious over him, with his cleansings and healings. Perchance, the one above, has still not forgiven him; he begins to think of a harsh punishment to be meted out to Pa Joe Joe – Hmmm! he says pondering a bit. Then his face lights up like a thousand-watt bulb. If Pa Joe Joe was not good enough for the **'ONE ABOVE'**, he leaving him to lie in his grave. He too would leave him there, never to rise again! Still enraged, the deceitful one disappears even faster than he came.

~~~

The Young One through her tears is looking at his blinking unseeing eyes and quivering lips – his lips quivering as if wanting to say something to her. Still kneeling at his bedside; She begins to tenderly trace the outlines of his face with a caressing finger – his eyes begin to flutter like wings of a dying butterfly or bee.
~~~

She then cups his face in her hands hoping to blunt any discomfort his tossing head might cause him. Weakly he says, *"It's alright lil one ah'm goin to a better place."* Then he promises. *"Anytime you need me I'll be dere for yuh, yes even in America – yuh got to go dere lil one, yuh Ma Jo Jo, she should have gone too, every ting woulda been so different, turned out better for her – I'm so sorry* **lil one**.*"* Then there is silence, he, listening for her reply – even for a sharp retort, a rebuke even.

His breaths are coming in short choked spurts; *"You do trust, yuh Pa Joe Joe, yuh* **'Gramps'** *don't you cakes? 'Cakes', 'Cakes,'* he breathes, now using his and her nicknames. She kisses his forehead for an answer, her tears flowing anew, on hearing the long-defeated sigh as his Head falls lifelessly out of her hands. The woman in New York had interrupted her life yet again.

Chapter 11

Ma Jo Jo is startled by the ruckus going on in the *'chicken run'* – she is concerned, didn't she secure all the fowls? Yes positively, even the ducks and two turkeys, she had locked in some borrowed fowl coops. Ma Jo Jo stops dead in her tracks as she listens to the rising fear in the screeches and cackles of her birds – those rarely heard sounds. Was that mongoose still trying to get to her fowls? She begins to replay her earlier moments in the fowl run and breathes evenly once again, being *cocksure* that all the fowls were in their coops, which she had latched securely. Now another thing she is certain about; She is not going out there, *'not for **all the tea in China**!'*

She repairs to the kitchen and pours herself a large cup of water, from the pitchoil tin that's seated on the oilcloth covered wooden table, that Pa Joe Joe had built himself. She sips slowly at the water in the large enamel cup. Now, the sudden increase in the frightened sounds coming from her caged birds are making Ma Jo Jo *'jittery'*. The nervous woman begins to rearrange her plastic vase of croton and hibiscus stems that she had placed therein just a few hours earlier. The fowls would have to deal with the storm as every other *'manjack'*, everyone was doing right now! Ma Jo Jo knowing ***full well*** that the outside would not be seeing her face on a night like this, ***"Every zandouille and mongoose will find their own hole tonight,"*** She affirms with a nervous little laugh then, ***"tonight, every pot has to sit on its own bottom,"*** she adds for good measure and convulses in gales of maddening laughter.

Yet again, Ma Jo Jo's house is shaken to its very foundation as the thunder roars across the heavens in quick succession, followed by the lightning, brightening up her drawing room as if on a normal sunny day. She is listening to the squealing of her pigs and the increase in the clucking of her fowls. Now she smells the flesh, the roasted flesh of a pig. One of her pigs is gone, taken by the lightning.

Ma Jo Jo sits down heavily at the table, her head resting on the pretty eye-catching lace tablecloth, the one that she had placed there over two weeks ago and overlayed with a clean plastic one. This tablecloth which she uses on special occasions, is still there on the table because some mourners were still coming by to pay their respects to the bereaved. The hypocrites! They, having despised or ignored her for over forty years, forty years!

What or to whom were they now displaying their misplaced sorrow and pity. They might as well continue going to the cemetery to cry out their anguish to the dead and buried Pa Joe Joe. She, having seen them at his gravesite on her way to and from her half-day servant job, with the *Dentist family* in the city, which she had acquired since Pa Joe Joe's death.

Ma Jo Jo is no fool, she knows that all this display of sorrow was not about her but the legend of Pa Joe Joe which is spread far and wide. Yes, the faith that these people had in him was still drawing them to his home and church out in the backyard. She has seen them reverently touching the balusters that he would hold onto on his way to the pulpit, they touching the walls and each vying for a seat on the wooden high chair under the starch mango tree, where he would sit while having his early morning coffee. These people really holding him in high esteem and reverence. Ma Jo Jo shudders inwardly – soft mournful sounds from deep within her weary soul emits her mouth, as she maybe for the hundredth time, mulls over his last days … …

The busybody Mother Gloria, fussing over the already perfectly arranged flowers or buffing the glistening brass pots, whenever there was a lull of foot traffic in the room. Ma Jo Jo, from time to time gets up from her chair in the corner of the room: She too, taking advantage of the lull and from behind her protective cover of the drape covered door, peeps at the overflowing crowds, some seated on the wooden benches brought out from inside the church, others on improvised seats, with slabs of wood atop of turned down buckets and pans. Even her *now* all too willing neighbors, lent their available chairs and small kitchen tables where their previously held pitchoil and cooking oil cans of clean water and one burner stoves would usually sit. Ma Jo Jo sighs knowing that with the expected influx of more visitors, a truck load or two of chairs and tables would have to be rented from a business in one of the nearby towns.

On hearing the disquieting grumbles coming from below her, she quietly takes a peek at those seated on the crowded steps. She knows that the steps leading to her drawing room, from where the visitors enter the house to offer Pa Joe Joe words of encouragement or to silently bid adieu, is just as likely crowded. The grumbling stems from those seated there and hate the disruptions or inconvenience of having to shift or get up, if someone was not willing to wait and would announce arrogantly that they wanted to **'pass'**, that they are on their way to **see** Pa Joe Joe.

<center>~~~</center>

Ma Jo Jo is deep in thought, dredging up the past and going over the Young Ones interaction with Pa Joe Joe on his deathbed...She was sitting unobtrusively in her corner as the Young One came in to see Pa Joe Joe, who then knelt by his bedside without taking a look around and Ma Jo Jo took that opportunity to slip out the room through the door that is also accessible to the church. Ma Jo Jo was standing behind that draped door peeping at the interaction between the Young One and Pa Joe Joe or rather the Young One's interaction, since Pa Joe Joe was once more lying prone on the bed, with her, the Young One holding his hand and whispering in his ear.

Ma Jo Jo sighs were followed by a series of tear-jerking sounds as she cradled her belly. This she has been doing relatively often and especially whenever her thoughts are on the Older One in America, whom she had not seen in the past three years. Ma Jo Jo knew that this was due to her father, who is barely getting around, even with the use of a cane and is solely dependent on her.

Then Ma Jo Jo glimpsed the Young One's impassive face as she suddenly got up, threw open the door and exited Pa Joe Joe's room, fleeing to her sanctuary, the river. She did not have to say not one word as she ran past. The shouts and drums rolls answered her silence. She heard the blood curdling wail of Ma Jo Jo behind her but did not move one muscle in its direction – not turning her head to so primal a scream that had some in the neighborhood running in its direction.

Yes, it was Ma Jo Jo cowering behind the black draped door to the church. Others sat stoically just where they were, and wondering about its authenticity. Why now, why now that he is dead? Everybody knew of their loveless but polite marriage. The *hoity toity* in the crowd sniffed their annoyance of her *low-class* behavior. What would Pa Joe Joe have thought about a scream so rabid, animalistic and undignified, coming from Ma Jo Jo who never showed any of this latent emotion for him.

Ma Jo Jo now on her knees, begins to sway as if in a faint. With tears pouring down her cheeks, she moans and laments while her hands protectively cradles her belly. The sounds pouring out of her are of regret and defeat. The life once full of promise that was taken away from her, through Pa Joe Joe's lost five years, is now being flaunted in her face.

Ma Jo Jo, still locked in the unforgiving past, is screaming louder and uglier. The screams are full of anger and fear too. She sees him, Joseph Celestine looking down in terror at the horror that's about to be perpetuated on her, them? She's warning him to get away from her, least he be destroyed too, just as she's about to be. The seemingly ugly and sweaty face bearing down on her; His salty beads of sweat falling on her face are nestling in her eyes, blotting out the vision, the last view of her innocent world. Might as well, since she does not wish to see his yellowed teeth, his ugly smile, the urgency on his face as he drunkenly tears into her, literally tearing her world apart.

~~~
~~~

Now, Ma Jo Jo, limping out of the church in search of the Young One, is being cryptically observed by the man of the mountain; His face hidden by the piece of flannelette draped over his head to protect him from catching a cold from the falling dew, it being way into the early morning.

The old man who is revered in the villages far and wide and is all of ninety-eight years, worries that with Pa Joe Joe gone, his followers would once again turn to him for their spiritual and medicinal needs. The old man slowly removes his clasps hands from between his knees – they begin to shake violently, so too does the knees that are hidden within the very wide legs of his flannel pants. The old man knows that he cannot do it anymore. He worries that when he too, like Pa Joe Joe is gone and that might be soon, that there would be no one of consequence to practice the craft, or if anyone did, he prays that it would not be purely for monetary gains. The old man makes an attempt, in fact several, to go over to Ma Jo Jo but realizes that his mind is willing, but his body just won't get off the bench.

Ma Jo Jo, whose eyes are no longer in search of the Young One who has disappeared among the tall bushes to the river, now seems to be captivated by the pulsating beats of the bongo drum and its lone drummer.

Ma Jo Jo is deeply immersed in the past; This is evident by the dance she is now executing and the drummer expertly tapping on the drum placed between his knees is keenly looking at her. Ma Jo Jo's dance is relative to every tap or pound on the drum. In essence, the drummer is talking to Ma Jo Jo, talking with his fingers on the drum. The villagers are mesmerized by Ma Jo Jo and the drummer, as they feed off each other. Even the young professional dancers who have come to entertain the crowd, stand aside, completely enthralled by this woman who it is being whispered amongst the awed crowd, had never danced this type of dance before. This is the woman their mamas, their *'nennens'* and the older neighbors often whispered about and not in a good way!

Ma Jo Jo is in a frenzy and no longer under the command of the drummer and his drum. Ma Jo Jo moves like a *jammette'*, worse than the village *'jagabat'* Claudine, that loose woman, drunk and *'wining'* in a band on Jouvert morning.

All through their life they have been hearing about this woman but only in gibberish; few of the words they understanding. Often, the adults would shout laughingly to one another, ***"little jackasses have big ears"***, to alert each other that a child or children were around and might be listening in on their adult conversation. Often times they would be talking about Ma Jo Jo and her husband; To be sure, most times they would be **bad talking** Ma Jo Jo – ill speak Pa Joe Joe they would never do!

Ma Jo Jo's footwork comes to a sudden stop, as if frozen in the last frame. She is back to it again; The quiet moans gliding out from between her partially closed lips; The involuntary swaying, the shuddering of her shoulders as if caught up in an unexpected cold snap – she slumps to the ground.

Ma Jo Jo is reliving a chapter of her life twenty-two years ago ... She's watching the village midwife delivering yet another of the hundreds by her hands. She is delivering Ma Jo Jo's grandchild. The mother, the Older One now queasy and uneasy at the moment, is wondering what on earth she has gotten herself into; Wondering and hoping that her plans of going to America to join him who really needs her, would not be thwarted by this ***thing*** that's happening to her.

On the emergence of the child and its subsequent cleansing, Ma Jo Jo steps forward, excitedly receives the child and lift it to the heavens in Thanksgiving. Then, even before the mother has the opportunity to hold her child, Ma Jo Jo is off to Pa Joe Joe, who is seated on his favorite cane bottomed chair at the front door, the curtain thrown over the door so as not to bother him, by ***blowing*** in his face or the pipe stuck in his mouth.

Ma Jo Jo hopes that his narrowed eyes are due to the smoke from his pipe, having heard him complaining about the green ***tobacco***. She reaches out to him, offering him the newborn. Ma Jo Jo sees the tightening and fast twitching of his jaw. They are both looking into each other's pained eyes, they, both wanting to hold on, crushing each other; Bodies melding into one, if that would only wash away the pain of those years. Now quickly, Pa Joe Joe averts his eyes but not quickly enough, before she sees the irreparable hurt and anger.

He shakes his head saying **no** and storms off to the river. He will not accept the Young One either. He does not want to love her, as he is already unknowingly doing. Ma Jo Jo feels the dagger like stab of pain to her heart – the painful lurching of her belly, caused by his rejection of yet another one. This one she wrongfully surmises, has nothing to do with their regretful past and present too.

Ma Jo Jo now sighs, she could never blame Pa Joe Joe for how their lives turned out – it would forever be her fault! She should have turned him away after their life changing five years apart – in essence, set him free.

Ma Jo Jo steps back into the bedroom, clothed in shame. Pa Joe Joe has rejected her one more time, but this time through the Young One. Both women's eyes are fixated on her; the one who has just given birth, snorts scornfully at her. Shamefacedly Ma Jo Jo looks at her, on seeing the fleeting pain in her eyes. Ma Jo Jo sighs, guess she is remembering how she too, was ripped away and sent to live with the old woman up the hill. Why won't they understand that her life was not hers, it was taken away the day that Pa Joe Joe was sent to prison. That she really owed hers to Pa Joe Joe – everything, for destroying his.

Tears begin to trickle down Ma Jo Jo's cheeks as the Older One who has just given birth snorts again and turns her back on the three in the room. Yes, even on the newborn, now being nestled against Ma Jo Jo's breasts. With her eyes fixated on the floor, the midwife takes her leave. This was their **kangkalang** – their melodrama – she had come and finished what she was called to do, delivering the Young One.

~~~

Finally, with the will power from within, the old man bested his failing body. Trembling fiercely and leaning on his walking stick, he gets up and shuffles over to Ma Jo Jo. The old man of the mountain aches all over, his every joint and even his meager flesh aches too!
~~~

He has been sitting on the straight back cane chair for far too long – even with the firm cushion under his bottom.

He reaches over with his stick, prodding the still writhing woman on the ground and nearly topples over but manages just in time to right himself. It is way past his bedtime and he is clearly exhausted. These past few days have been rigorous; Because of his standing in the community of spiritual leaders, everything pertaining to the last days leading up to the funeral of the revered Pa Joe Joe, is left up to him. He is thankful to the leaders who are temporarily residing in the church outback, who readily follows through with any and all the duties he delegates to them.

The old man of the mountain, is also overburdened by the vast numbers of apologetic people who keep coming up to him, laying their problems *'at a time like this'* on him, their words; but believe that their problem to be a life-or-death situation. That there was no other to dispense their bush medicine and their bush bath potions with Pa Joe Joe gone.

The old man is deeply troubled and concerned for those who can be gullible to those ***'fly by night'*** medicine men springing up all over the villages. He begins to think about the times he sent away some of the villagers with their prized concoctions without taking a farthing, not one penny, even for the ingredients used, knowing that they could barely afford the money offered.

The two temporary leaders in the church outback, have been keenly eyeing the old man of the mountains and now move closer to him – one standing on either side. The old man keeps a sympathetic eye on the woman on the ground as her writhing and moaning has been somewhat contained. For all the years that he had known her, he pauses and corrects himself, **seen her**, for that what it was. He having seen and said very few words to her on her sporadic visits to the newly released from prison, Joseph Celestine who lived for a short time in his mountaintop home.

He shakes his head with regret, as he recalls the many times that he would advise Joseph Celestine not to marry the young woman. He did not want to tell him plainly, that he should spare her from the prison that he was about to shut her into, just as he was released from his. The wise old man of the mountain knew too, that Joseph

Celestine unfairly blamed her, for what had happened to both their lives.

The young man was adamant, unreasonably so. They would be together forever; They had made that promise to their teenage selves and so it would be – till death would they part! The man of the mountain noted that he hadn't said anything about love. He also noticed the desperate cry for help, the tumultuous sea of pain, followed by the raging burning fire of fear and that he also saw the underlying dark hatred deep within his eyes.

He bends as low as his aching back would allow. He touches her shoulders – Ma Jo Jo now in a sitting position, feels it immediately; Soft, soothing, healing, she wishes that it would tell her that he really still loved her; Her Pa Joe Joe did.

Ma Jo Jo moans, looks up into the stern yet understanding face of the man. With the crock of his finger, he motions her to get up from the ground, which she does somewhat shamefacedly, quickly disappearing into the house. Now, the two priests move in and gently steady the old man on his feet, guiding him to another comfortable chair.

The plush plump cushioned rocking chair, that they guided him to, once seated the behind of the Irish woman's husband. This chair, she humbly donated, paying homage to Pa Joe Joe for the **good works** that he has done, whatever those *'good works'* were. She only knew that her servants, the washerwoman/ironer, Rosita and house cleaner Gemma, would speak reverently of him and his works. "Mumbo Jumbo", she would whisper into the telephone when speaking back home to Ireland, about Pa Joe Joe and the villagers.

Though, she nor her dead husband actively participated in the villagers way of life, they were always helpful and respectful – keenly aware that the majority of the able-bodied villagers in their employ, were the lifeline of their holdings, their vast cocoa and coconut estates that her husband once managed then eventually owned.

~~~
~~~

Pa Joe Joe's wake is in full swing, the drummers going at it with much zeal and gusto. Unlike the previous night when the lone drummer was low keyed, as if not wanting to hurry the already dead, great Pa Joe Joe home.

Elvin and his boys were enlisted by his father to help in building a covered stage, something they were contemplating anyway, ever since being told that Pa Joe Joe had begun his journey to the **other side**. On completion of the stage and seating the steel chairs there on, Elvin and his friends, found themselves in the same position as most of the villagers – relegated to standing at the fringes. They impassively looking on at those self-important outsiders, hypocrites, the purposefully *late commers*, especially the would-be politicians who were hoping to catch the eyes and impress the mammoth crowd upon their late arrival!

The benches were taken out of Pa Joe Joe's church and long occupied by the ***early birds***, some there since the night before and only leaving their seats, if sat on by a friend or relative with an assurance that it would be given up, when they returned to the ***dead house*** after going home to *'wet dey skin'* with water, from their filled drums behind their homes or running down by the river for a ***quick dip*** to cleanse themselves. There are those who would do neither, knowing that the must have enamel cups of coffee would be passed around, followed by a substantial meal at the appropriate time.

As the wake progressed, so did the crowd in size, that a small section with chairs and benches previously lent by neighbors, were designated only seating for the elderly, infirmed, pregnant women, or those with small children in tow.

~~~

Now, Ma Z looks up at the darkening skies, deciding then and there, not to leave the comfort of her house to go down to the wake – a place where her presence, might encourage more ***tankalang***, more gossip. Then, she looks lower down the hill to Ma Jo Jo's house that appears to be in danger of being overrun, swallowed up by the multitudes surrounding it. Some young men are trying to impress the girls, by loosely hanging from the trees nearby –
~~~

dangerously swinging from branch to branch, making Tarzan like noises just like in the movies. Others sitting on said branches, breezily swinging their feet and eating the ripened fruits. Farther afield, the younger and lithe boys on the guava and cashew trees are having a fruit fight, tossing their half-eaten fruit at each other.

Ma Z keeps searching the crowd in the hope of catching a glimpse of Ma Jo Jo. She has heard that three of Pa Joe Joe's childhood best friends had arrived. Amongst them his very best friend and rival at everything – even sports, **_Gold Teeth_**. She steupsed at the idea of the name, **_Gold Teeth_**. Anyway, on not seeing any sign of *'her'* in the crowd, she hopes that Ma Jo Jo would keep her *'ole tail'* quiet and inside her house. She hadn't seen them either; The men being excitedly talked about, who was said to be freely spending on the drinks and food for the wake.

On hearing the shouts and squeals of terror from the crowd Ma Z squints and follows their gaze up into the trees. She could see some of the young men with arms outstretched standing on the swaying branches; *'performing'* for the young girls. Ma Z grumbles with annoyance, sure that the girls were looking at the fools; their *hands* covering their *faces*, with their fingers splayed to get a look – at the performance no matter how disgusting.

<div align="center">~~~</div>

"Long time no see! Long time no see! Long time no see!", come the effusive greetings; this is followed by a loud roar, that was always his laughter. *"Back at you, back at you, long time no see to you too!"*, comes the reply. It is *him*, he has finally appeared to the crowd. Ma Z squints at the three men standing by themselves; The tall one in the banlon jersey that barely fits his massive chest; she assumes, is the one called **_Big Chest_**. The second one, has heads and the chatter turned way up. He is tall, really tall and standing under one of the trees, his head seeming to be swallowed up in the low hanging branches of the zaboca tree, admittedly one of the shorter trees though.

The circus has come to town – the young men purposely walking near to this one, comparing heights. Suddenly, he grabs at

Elvin lifting him off the ground and for a few seconds has his feet dangling in midair, much to the delight of the crowd – this one is called *Tallest* – the bearer of two unusually large feet, who is also snidely called *Foots* behind his back, by friends and foes alike. Heck, in times past he used those feet with aplomb – weapons, during a fight and getting the desired results; foes, even with weapons in hand running away or surrendering. The appearance of the third one, quickly brings an end to the hilarity; He has both hands outstretched, tempering down the crowd in an attempt to bring back the solemnity of its purpose.

Ma Z gives this one a good looking over; Even though it is well over forty years, she would recognize him anywhere. Like Pa Joe Joe his rival and yet, best friend he was still handsome. Now he smiles, his smile wide, teeth gleaming. Back then, in their childhood, his friends did call him *Gold Teeth*, though he did not possess them. His teeth always white and nearly sparkling, he, always chewing on a *Datwon* his toothbrush of choice, made of a twig of the hibiscus plant, that some thought, makes one's teeth clean and sparkling bright; though that did not justify him being called Gold Teeth. Nevertheless, it made sense to him and his friends when as a young boy, he'd take the gold-colored wrapper from his candy and secure it on his upper front teeth.

Ma Z would have grimaced in horror on seeing him now with true, true gleaming gold teeth in place of his pulled natural pearly whites. Still she would have exclaimed, *'Gold Teet'* mih foot; He was Clyde then and will always *be – Clyde* to her.

"Ah Hope he didn't pull out he good, good teet', to put in dem damn fool things", she asserted before slamming her door shut – still hoping that Ma Jo Jo would keep her *'tail'* in the house and that the three men whom she really loved in their youth, would leave as soon as the funeral was over and *that one* in particular would not further complicate Ma Jo Jo's life.

Quickly shutting the door, Ma Z stops dead in her tracks, deeply conflicted – going back and forth on her decision to stay indoors. Maybe she should go down there right now, to protect that damn fool of a vulnerable woman! She peeps through the cracks of a wooden window – at the massive crowd that is spilling over, swallowing up the neighboring yards on both sides of Ma Jo Jo's.

Ma Z shakes her head no! With definite finality – she would not make an appearance and *raise the dead*, the rumors of what she was blamed for over forty years ago, and still not forgotten nor forgiven. Let it stay buried with Pa Joe Joe now on top of it. Her last fervent hope is that Ma Jo Jo would not make a showing until the day of the funeral.

Ma Jo Jo herself, not wanting to be made a ***pappy show***, a laughingstock, is a no show on the stage, on one of the seats allotted for the dead man's family members. She knows that it would happen, that someone in the multitude of people would point her out, bringing up the long past bacchanal, making her a spectacle anew. So, with a keen eye, she takes in the proceedings from behind the black drape covering the doorway.

Ma Jo Jo is looking at the defiant looking Older One who is sitting there on stage but only after making it clear, that she is not there as a family member to take part in anything, but to give comfort to the Young One who loved Pa Joe Joe dearly and while putting on a brave, face she is deeply affected by his passing. The Older One also made it known, that as soon as all this foolishness was over, she would be flying back to New York where she was loved and desperately needed.

From behind the black drape in her bedroom, Ma Jo Jo keeps her wary eyes both on the stage and the trace leading to the river. She, anxiously looking out for the Young One, who since Pa Joe Joe's death is going there frequently and spending longer and longer alone times there.

She anxiously begins shifting from one foot to the other. This anxiety is due to what Elvin reported on the conversation that he and the Young One shared about her fascination with the river. Ma Joe Joe comforts herself, that for the day, she had not yet seen the Young One, or rather her large afro hairdo over the tops of the tall bushes and reeds as she trots along the trace to the river.

Sick with worry the day before, Ma Jo Jo had sent Elvin after the Young One on her sojourn to the river, warning him to keep to the bushes least she might think him spying on her. Then too, Ma Jo Jo is aware that like most of the young men in the neighborhood, Elvin too, was *'sweet'* on the Young One who has blossomed into a very attractive young woman and was doing her very best in keeping the bothersome young village boys at bay. She was already enamored with the University educated young man of the city, he with the putt, putt, putt Motorbike and he clearly with her. She had also become immersed with quite a divergent group in the city – steeped in politics and the awakening to *their culture* and heritage but yet tapping heavily in the politics and culture from abroad – America really. Whenever this was pointed out to these highly aroused youths, they would simply state that, *"All ah we is one"*, coming from one family, straight out of Africa. The village had clearly lost her, or strangely, was she ever one with them?

Ma Jo Jo smiled, sadly thinking that the village was indeed changing. Oh, how she wishes for the days when predictably the electricity would shut off as most of the households were watching the six O'clock news on their TV sets, while having their *'tea'*, their dinners.

She's remembering too, the Saturday mornings when the Young Ones, home from school or work and listening to their music with the radios turned way way up, as the DJs cranked out their favorite pop song or calypso, the anguished and frustrating shouts of, *'current gone!' 'current gone!'* Would be heard echoing around the neighborhood. Ma Jo Jo filled with nostalgia, wonders where to and when did those years pass by.

Ma Jo Jo once again begins focusing on the trace leading to the river, hoping to catch a glimpse of the large afro, bouncing over the tall bushes on her way back from the river or, as she would conspiratorially whisper to Miss Cedeno, Elvin's Ma, about the Young One and her companions hair style, *'upside down mops in dashikis and sandals.'* Then they would both collapse in laughter.

Ma Jo Jo's eyes seek out the Older One seated in the front of the crowded stage. Her arms are folded defiantly across her chest – her thimble heel wearing feet, planted firmly on the floor. She, definitely sending out a *don't give it damn message*. Ma Jo Jo behind her drape, tries hard to suppress the stream of giggles flowing from a place she could not contain. Maybe the Older One was channeling her ten-year-old self and her cries of protest as she received a proper **cutail**, her *'behind'* getting a proper **washing**, yet another beating, with that piece of Pa Joe Joe's broken belt, on Ma Jo Jo getting yet another complaint of the Older One's *womanish* ways, her belligerence to an elder of the neighborhood.

Did she make a **monkey face**, gave a **cokey eye**? Her crossed eyes were certainly the fiercest among her friends. Maybe too, she had steupsed – sucked her teeth, or shaken her *tail*, her behind, at an elder, these last two, definitely no no's, highly disrespectful!

"Dey was bad talking yuh," she would cry out in protest, but not in pain from Ma Jo Jo's hand or the broken belt – she just could not understand why Ma Jo Jo was administering a beating on her when all she was doing was sticking up for her against those who were **washing their mouths** on her, definitely ill speaking her.

Ma Jo Jo gulps in disbelief as the Older One is reverting to her ten-year-old self, displaying her trick faces to the adults in the mammoth crowd, whom she believes is spreading ugly rumors about Ma Jo Jo. Ma Jo Jo is filled with anxiety at the Older One's action and not being out there in the wake, thinks it wise to depart from hiding behind the black drape so she repairs to the kitchen where she makes herself a **strong** hot cup of lime bud tea.

~~~

Pa Joe Joe is about to get a great send off, one befitting a man such as he – a King! His friends from the city determined that this was how it is going to be. Immediately on their arrival back in the village, the three went to his bedside paying their respect – each with his own private thoughts – no doubt, their youthful exploits together, a major apart. They had arrived in their head turning and eye-popping red sports car; hood down. Pa Joe Jo would have roared with laughter at their presentation. Gold Teeth the driver, had one hand on the steering wheel, the other, stretched out the window, chunky gold rings adorning each of his splayed fingers. Yes, even the thumb, gleaming in the morning sun.
~~~

One of his ***riding*** partners in the front seat next to him, held the same posture arm stretched way out of the car window – rings, on fingers gleaming in accordance. Not to be outdone was their backseat driver, Tallest. In a straight case of ***'monkey see, monkey do,'*** Tallest had his hand positioned likewise, his ***silver*** rings on each of his four fingers, the lone gold one on his thumb; To be sure, he was holding his own, in the vanity department.

Tallest, had been ***getting on their nerves***, directing Gold Teeth, telling him when to ***'mash'*** brakes, slow down, speed up, but worst of all was his sending them in wrong directions, ending up in dead end tracks and twice being stuck in muddy puddles. Gold Teeth, angry at having to watch his previously clean and shiny car, splattered with mud on its tires and caked in said mud. Their travails coming to an end, when again on the insistence of Tallest, they took a wrong turn, nearly catapulting in a ravine – his final mistake.

He Tallest, was on the verge of being tossed into the ravine himself but was saved by Big Ches', who with a wide grin and mischievous smile in his eyes, drew Gold Teeth's attention to the abandoned dented bucket, trapped and bobbing between two large stones in the water, then to a maybe forgotten piece of clothing on some bushes, he pointed to Tallest. Gold Teeth roared with laughter and as if in a simulated act they both pointed to Tallest, showing him the abandoned articles, and then at the mud-splattered car – Tallest understood.

Happy to be back in the good graces of his two friends he quickly slipped off his brown *'jim boots'*, rolled up the legs of his pants and was soon having a go at the mud-splattered car. Nearby, Big Ches' and Gold Teeth were making fun of him as they pelted him with the peels of the ripe mangoes they were rapturously enjoying.

Yes, there they all stood at Pa Joe Joe's bedside, barely breathing themselves, as if in fear of waking him. Gold Teeth Was standing there, looking down at the friend of his youth, when friends and friendships really mattered. He knew that even if he kept standing there until ***cock get teeth***, forever more, he would never understand this thing called death, as his departed friend most certainly must have done. So, he nudged the two others and they suddenly backed away from his bedside, replacing their *stingy brimmed* hats on their heads, only after completely backing all the way out of the room.

Gold Teeth had done that, coordinated their head gear, in paying homage to him with their *'stingy brimmed'* hats, a new trend that Pa Joe Joe never wore but which the young Joseph Celestine most certainly would have worn.

A harsh angry glint came to Gold Teeth's eyes, his jaws began to twitch rapidly as he skipped over the five steps to the yard and stormed off to sit in the cooling air, the two others following meekly.

Gold Teeth, Pa Joe Joe's best friend and sometimes rival, was left alone with his thoughts. He had left him, his famous friend and the village, to seek his own brand of fame and fortune! The village was his friend Joseph's to explore and explode, via the track and field also. There was that formidable rock over the waterfall, that he, Gold Teeth had to get away from. The streams, rivulets, the bamboo patches, the nightly hunts, those things were strangling him – holding him down.

He was tired of sitting at the side of the dirt tracks and traces in the mornings, with his favorite caged bird at his feet, as he contemplated what other tree he was going to bleed off it's *'milk'* to make the *'laglee'*, the glue to stick on a tree, in hopes of catching the elusive bird that he had spotted deep in the forest.

Truth be told, he was tired of trapping birds; also, he needed to set free those in the cages that he had trapped overtime. Then, to free himself of his own cage – this village.

On hearing the waterfall in the distance, Gold Teeth breathes out sharply, as if trying to rid himself of its taunting sounds; Yet another of the things that he ran away from invading his psyche, as it is presently doing, dragging him back into the past ...He's on the second tier of the treacherous rock leading to the waterfall. His friend Joseph Celestine, already having accomplished the feat of surmounting and conquering the rock, is standing on its very top, his arms akimbo on his lean narrow hips, is looking imperiously down on him and laughing good naturedly.

Clyde, for that is his name but not what he was called back then; had struggled mightily to get to the point where he then triumphantly stood, so as not to get the full good natured ribbing that he surely would have gotten if failing to scale any part of the rock. Midway in the climb he had decided not to try anymore.

Then and there he decided that scaling the waterfall was not worth it – falling to his death. There had to be much more outside the village, which he now must get away from.

~~~

Standing on the sideline of the vast crowd in Pa Joe Joe's wake and through the haze of cigarette smoke that is being exhaled, Gold Teeth, Clyde, sees the real reason why he left the village, moving from behind the black draped doorway and descending the stairs.

Gold Teeth sighs, digs his hand into his pocket, and takes out a wad of cash, which he wordlessly hands over to Big Ches'. This is the second such wad that he has taken out since coming back to the village. The first one meant to be spent on the *'jorts'*, all the food needed for this massive crowd, he had given to Elvin and one of the charming young ladies.

That particular **_charming young lady_** seemed to be *'sweet'* on Big Ches', undeniably a magnificent specimen of a human being, who in the few hours of his arrival, had most of the available ladies of the village vying for his attention, flaunting their **wares** before him.

From the hilltop, the appetizing scents pervading the air are coming from the large iron pots, filled with all types of ground provisions and wild meats, each pot atop three large stones stacked with wood of all kinds beneath them and a raging *'fire ago'*.

Gold Teeth turns around annoyed, as he feels the hand tugging at his shoulder. **_"Aye man, she gone dong dere, dong by de ole Canyon"_**, Elvin flatly informs him, a broad knowing smile, plastered on his face, as he points toward the forest, covered in a thick blanket of blackness. He, Elvin, hoping that the *city man*, Gold Teeth, has notice that he had used the **big word**, Canyon, though
~~~

incorrectly, instead of simply stating that she had *gone down by de river*. Gold Teeth notices, shakes his head and smiles at Elvin's reference to Ma Jo Jo and him. So, the gossip mongers are at it once again – they never forgot or leave it alone, whether wrong or right, don't they?

Despite the flashlight in his hand, Gold Teeth stumbles along the path to the river. He has stayed away much too long – he would rectify that, he swears to himself. Stumbling along, he slips on a half-eaten mango and nearly ends up in a *'picker patch'*. He breathes a sigh of relief, knowing that had he done so, the results would have been very painful, with the thorns of those bushes tearing into his flesh.

He looks up into the sky or is it *into heaven* in reference to Pa Joe Joe's new abode. He is sure that Pa Joe Joe is doubling up with laughter as they often did at each other's follies. As he huffs and puffs, sometimes holding onto his chest and stumbling along the forgotten terrain, he could see his yesterday's unreeling before him ...

There's Pa Joe Joe, no, the young Joseph Celestine atop the waterfall; Tall and lean, clad in torn shirt and ragged khaki pants. This time his hand is over his mouth, least the laughter that's deep down within his soul comes roaring out filling up the forest, floating up to the heavens on the buoyant clouds and then tumbling down the roaring waterfall, riding on the ripples in the pond embarrassing his now panting friend – Clydie to him.

Gold Teeth, angry at his stumblings and at his having to grasp at the bushes to steady himself, is also imagining his rival laughing off his head at him. He decides to get back at him the only way open to him now – through his Josephine. He has to quiet his mocking laughter once and for all. He veers off the known and reliable trace, taking a *short cut* through a more treacherous one where it would take him half the time to get to the river, and maybe to her.

Like a drunken man, he stumbles ahead in the bushes, clawing his way through the entangling wild vines, that's doing the same back at him, clawing; tearing at his clothes and flesh. He stops suddenly and listens. He clearly hears the roar of the rushing water and realizes that he was making his way up hill all this time. Properly winded, he decides to stay put a while and catch his breath, his hands on his throbbing knees.

Feeling an eerie yet familiar presence he looks clear up the hill, to the waterfall. There he stands on the second tier of the rock, his rock. A slow and quiet chuckle escapes Gold Teeth, which grows into a tremendous roar. He has come down to meet him – the rivalry is now completely over.

Gold Teeth straightens up – He is dressed in the finest of robes bright and gleaming as if lit with hundreds of bulbs. Gold Teeth, now stands up to his full height – they look at each other and roar. Their laughter like thunder, screaming across the skies, like earthquakes shaking the earth. *'He'* expands his arms – the birds from their childhood flying to him, nestling thereon.

Astonished, Gold Teeth Is having difficulty in breathing, the man is still on the second tier of the gigantic rock. Then, every bird that had eluded him, that he Gold Teeth ever dreamt of trapping in his youth, flies right to him , tweeting and whistling – Gold Teeth lifts his hand, touching those most sought after birds – none flies away. Again, Gold Teeth and his friend look at each other breaking out in simultaneous rip-roaring laughter – their laughter screeching across the skies causing the stars to pitch every which way – a kaleidoscope of colors under the heavens.

His shoulders shaking uncontrollably, with fits of laughter and the freeing of long frozen emotional tears, Gold Teeth is slowly brought down to his knees. Now, completely released from his emotional baggage, he feels a gentle hand on his shoulder – he looks up into the kind understanding eyes of Ma Jo Jo – no longer anyone's Josephine – the rivalry is indeed over. He quickly and guiltily casts his eyes toward the second tier of the rock. The illuminating figure is not there anymore.

'He', the man who had lost five years of his youth, all the fame and fortune that could have encapsulated that life – a man who devoted the rest of his life to helping others, who lost the love of his life, even though she was right there beside him, willing to give him all the love that he needed and more.

Gold Teeth gets up from his knees, he isn't done with his friend yet. Tonight, would be the last night of his wake, tomorrow his funeral. Thinking of his apparition on the rock, Gold Teeth surmises that he is really a King and his end would thusly be befitting a King!

Gold Teeth, driven by a force that he didn't know he possessed, finds himself leaping over the big stones and felled trees in his way. No longer feeling the sting of the entangling grasses and bushes cutting into his flesh. He feels his heart pounding as if wanting to burst through his chest and his banlon Jersey.

Cutting through the bushes, he has left Ma Jo Jo behind. He would not go back there again; she is no longer the Josephine whom they both rivaled over. She had truly belonged to the one who should have been on the world stage – the sporting world stage, through his athleticism. Gold Teeth, stumbling along, hears the laughter behind him. His friend, rival of old, laughing uproariously at him, because he has forgotten how it was to be a village boy – but Gold Teeth would not be distracted – he has to get back there at the wake, has to honor him tonight.

Once again on joining the wake, Gold Teeth survey's the overflowing crowd, quickly moves to the outside, sticks the appropriate fingers in his mouth and blows in an out, hard! Resulting in the loudest attention-grabbing whistling sound. Big Ches' and Tallest are involved in their own conversation in another part of the yard with the young ladies whose rapt attention they have captured. The young ladies enthralled by these worldly men, each hoping to capture the attention and hearts of either of these men – their *'could be'* ticket out of the village.

The both men have heard Gold Teeth's familiar shrill whistle, summoning them and trots-over to him. Their ensuing conversation is both solemn and serious. The attendees of the wake are having their fill with food and drinks or as Elvin had wittingly put it, they were ***greedily feeding the holes beneath their noses***.

Gold Teeth is being briefed by his two friends, about the grumbling amongst some of the men of the village. Seems like the seasoned gamblers from within and outside of the village, those who would go from wake to wake, mostly for the illicit liquor, the

bush rum, most sought after for its potency. Those gamblers have seized the available bottles and stored them under their tables for their own enjoyment. Gold Teeth looks at his watch, whispers to his friends, then motions with his head to Elvin, who seems to be anxiously looking out for that signal, to come over.

Gold Teeth is behind the wheel of his red Motorcar with its hood down and there sits Elvin besides him in the front seat and his two friends in the back. Gold Teeth having left Big Ches' and Tallest behind to control things. Gold Teeth smiles at their antics knowing that they are aping him – Elvin and the two others. Their arms out the rolled down windows of the car, their fingers ringless, splayed. Sometimes trying to touch the squealing young ladies at the side of the road, excited to be seeing the young boys in a car such as this.

To the open mouthed '*gaping*' young men with their bird cages in their hands or pushing their box carts, with or without filled pans of water at this ugly hour of four thirty in the morning, Elvin and his two friends offer curt nods of their heads, then erupts in loud guffaws as soon as the car passes by and they are no longer in hearing range.

Gold Teeth glances across at Elvin once again – a hard cold look comes into his eyes. He is *seeing* himself before he had gotten rid of being just the ***village boy***! This boy should not be stagnated, becoming just another *village boy*, he thinks of Elvin.

He sighs, then takes a deep breath, he is becoming too fond of that boy. He has to leave him alone least he ends up in the same place as he and Pa Joe Joe, though for different things, different times – the end result, the same though – wasted years.

With his arm out the car, Gold Teeth keeps on flicking at the imaginary cigarette between his fingers – he needs one badly now. He again looks across at Elvin, sure enough Elvin is doing the same, flicking at the imaginary cigarette between his fingers.

Gold Teeth smiles inwardly; This is most certainly a case of ***monkey see monkey do***! He smiles broadly as another thought comes to his mind; ***You can take the boy out of the village, but never can you take the village out of the boy!*** With that he begins laughing hysterically – pounding on the steering wheel. He looks across at Elvin's puzzled face and says in a musical tonel *I'm just a village boy, lonely and blue*, a takeoff from the song *lonely boy* a popular song from his youth, the singer's name he cannot now recall.

Then doubling up with laughter, and pounding this time on the horn, he startles the people already at the side of the tracks, causing them to jump into the bushes as they look after the man in his big impressive red car, driving by with truly just a *village boy* sitting at his side.

~~~

Gold Teeth keeps on looking at the growing crowd which was already massive from the early evening. He is aware that it's the last night of the wake, some on the fringes, standing on benches, boxes, downturned galvanized buckets, anything, as long as they could get a good view of the front of the stage at the chanteuses and dancers all under the hypnotic spell of the thumping drums. These acts, byproducts of a wake such as this, which they all feverishly anticipated.

Angry shouts from those whose view are being blocked come fast and furious; *'Alyuh fadders is glass makers'*, is just one such angry and annoyed shout coming from the crowd. Gold Teeth and his friends laugh and laugh at the picong being hurled back and forth – most often, the lighthearted insults are being hurled for their benefit, those doing the *hurling* gratified by their delightful reactions; certain that the three men had not heard or had forgotten the picong's being tossed around and without the obscenities that might have been added in the city.

Gold teeth keeps on smiling – the broad smile, even crinkling the corners of his eyes. He looks up into the heavens; *If* he is up there, or if anybody really got there; Gold Teeth's breath is immediately caught in his throat. He knows better than to question or to use those *ifs*! His sainted parents were there! He knows that from his early teachings, he himself was once headed there ...where his friend is right now!
~~~

His mind begins to travel back into the distant past – searching, seeking. Then this disquieting feeling creeps into his being; He tries to chase it away, the feeling. Was his friend Joseph Celestine doing this to him again, brandishing the guilt card, for the way he is living his life, he wanting him to make the village his home once again? Gold Teeth is conflicted, he is being torn apart, receiving a *beating* at his friend's wake. He again walks away from the two others, Big Ches' and Tallest – it is all right, they know where he is headed.

Nearing the river, he looks up into the heavens and sees him immediately, just as he would see him in their youth; He Joseph, atop the waterfall, looking down at him, he who never cared to leave the first tier and rarely ascended to the second tier of the rock leading up to the waterfall.

Why was he doing this to him even now, brandishing, the guilty, the cowardice card? *"Pope! Pope! Pope!",* he calls out, astonished that the name with which only he called Joseph Celestine, teasing him in their youth, would tumble out. He doesn't flinch at the stern-faced vision of his friend – judgmental! Gold Teeth assumes. *"Pope! Pope!",* he again shouts at the fast-fading mirage of his friend over the waterfall and now heaven bound. He furtively looks around and then back up at the waterfall saying almost pleadingly, *"Ah know dat yuh can still show yuhself up dere, Pope now show yuhself to mih!"*

He pauses; now at the no show of his friend, he clears his throat saying fervently, *Aye Pope, dis is de Acolyte, ah know dat yuh want me to embarrass mihself wid dis name dat yuh give mih, right?* Gold Teeth is referring to the many times when not with Josephine, the Bible loving Joseph Celestine and himself would sit on the river's bank, bare feet dangling in the cooling and soothing waters of the river. There, Joseph Celestine would be espousing the verses of the Bible as he interpreted them. Poor *Clydie*, often peeved when not given a chance to get a word in edgewise, would spitefully call his friend Pope and he in turn would hit back, calling him Acolyte, the grudgingly accepted names amongst themselves.

Gold Teeth sighs and mumbles unapologetically, *"yuh know dat ah different now,"* he is referring to the life that he, began to live after leaving the village – the heavy drinking, the gambling, the owning and running of whore houses that led to his first stint in jail. Gold Teeth receives nothing but deathly silence.

Annoyed, he begins with his customary grinding of teeth and kicking at the pebbles with his brand-new ***kick and stab or pointy tipped shoes***, the foot – wear fashion statement of the day. Hopefully, he looks up to the heavens – though thinking that his friend Joseph, would spitefully not give him peace of mind by making an appearance.

Gold Teeth, deep in thought and with a quizzical look on his face stands there, rubbing his chin. Then a big old grin takes over his whole broad face. His teeth gleaming in the dark night, just like the sparks and embers flying high into the night, that escape from the fireside under the giant-sized bubbling pots of food, cooking on the nearby hill, away from the mourners.

Before leaving the riverside, Gold Teeth again looked up and saluted the heavens and if his gaze had lingered a little longer, he would have seen that big, beautiful star that seemed to pitch across the heavens in acknowledgement of his salutation.

Gold Teeth, back in the thick of the mourners, searching but not seeing his friends, does the next best thing; he crocks one of his fingers sticks its knuckle under his tongue and blows out, hard! The effort leaving his eyes bulging and the furrows on his forehead deepening. He is blowing out his frustrations, his dissatisfaction, of not finding the peace and answers that he needed from his dead friend.

~~~

The earsplitting attention grabbing sound barely leaving his lips, has every head turning in his direction. Big Ches' and Tallest exchange knowing glances, this is all about the best friend of his youth. They had noted his previous jaunts to the river and his demeanor on his return.

Gold Teeth then extends one long armed crimson clad jersey across his throat in a cutting motion. This gesture is directed to the drummers, dancers and the performers. The motion is understood.
~~~

Abruptly not a note or sound is heard from the performers but for those from the stray dogs. He dramatically makes his way to the center of the crowd. The mourners close by immediately begin peeling away, leaving him all alone. He looks toward the drummers, pointing a gleaming gold ringed finger straight at them, which starts the thumping of one lone drummer...Gold Teeth's movements begins slow, very slowly and wooden. He, again but now with the other hand, points another gold clamped ringed finger, resulting in the thumping of yet another drum. His pointy tipped shoes as if leaving trails in the dirt, with his wooden deliberate movements.

Gold Teeth then pounds his feet on the ground, simultaneously pumping his fists in the air and as if on cue, the rest of the drummers join in. The sweat is pouring down from his head into his eyes – he just keeps shaking off the streams of perspiration into the night air; Nothing must deter him from executing this dance, which is determined, angry and vengeful.

At the end of his performance, the preachers and the observants made up of mostly the elderly under the tent, make sure that their appreciation is noted by the enthusiastic applause. Gold Teeth is non-plussed, this is not what his performance was all about.

The now jaded man is drained of any emotion, he looks around at the crowd, a disparate one for the most part. The wayward children, the young men and women flaunting themselves at each other, some Older Ones wondering about their leaderless selves, what with Pa Joe Joe gone, the card players gambling and drinking heavily now. This too, is not about his friend anymore – scenes like these mean that things are out of control.

The older women had abandoned the cooking after the first chaotic night, knowing that the others to follow would be even more so. Elvin and his friends having haphazardly taken over, had become ***chief cooks and bottle washers*** leaving many to concur in amazement, that men really are the better cooks.

~~~

Big Ches' looks on, uncomfortable at the bond developing between Gold Teeth, Elvin and Elvin's hapless friend Carter. He is
~~~

sure that Gold Teeth is reliving his youth through the friend's antics. What did he want to do; Save them from themselves, what if they were happy just being *village boys*? Big Ches' and Tallest becoming concerned, uneasily shared their thoughts about their mentor, benefactor but most of all friend.

Gold Teeth is throwing unreadable glances at one of the tents – taking in the antics of the group of young men who have just moved in, their chores at the fireside on the hill completed. Bits and pieces of their conversation are floating out. Elvin flopping down on one of the steel chairs complaints loudly of being **ded out**, very tired.

Soon laughter erupts; drowning out the hoarse voice of the preacher man on the stage, who is extolling the virtues of the dead man: ***"like he eat plenty, plenty, ochroes or what; how come dem words jus slipping out he mout easy, easy so?"*** This was meant more as a statement than a question asked of the newly ordained pastor, who has high hopes of getting access to Pa Joe Joe's shuttered church. At this, the young men erupt in sidesplitting laughter, with each trying to outdo the other with their witticism.

The preacher man knowing that this is the last night of Pa Joe Joe's wake is on a roll. The crowd being very receptive of and *eating up* his fiery sermon. This he knows from the remarks he hears from time to time from those he truly moved: ***Preach brudderman! Tell dem like it is! Ehmm! Ahmm: Yes Lord! Amen, yuh preachin brudder!***

Now, the preacher man is annoyed at being interrupted by the coughing and choking sounds coming from someone standing on the fringe of the mammoth crowd and at every sound, he would hrrrmph! ***"A cigarette is a ball of fire with a jackass behind it!"*** This Elvin says beneath his breath. Those who hear him, respectfully says nothing, they understand that his anger and pain is directed to the ***'maga, maga man'***, the very thin man coughing and choking with the equally thin long cigarette still between his lips. That man is his uncle **Bo boy** whom the whole family was proud of, he being a nurse and a senior one at that, coming from a family of gardeners and field hands. He was also employed in the one and only hospital in the city. ***"An educated jackass!"*** Elvin adds as an afterthought as he looks at the man consumed with another fitful bout of coughing and sputtering, running off into the thickness of the black night where his sputtering and coughing could still be heard. This again comes angrily from Elvin; *Ah dying jackass too!* For he had heard this whispered by his relatives – *Cancer, Bo boy have cancer!* Elvin, not one to miss out on a good picong session, soon rejoins the jovial bunch. He, Carter and the rest of his friends being the masters of picong.

Gold Teeth with an amused smile shakes his head as he looks after the young man Elvin, now walking away with a plate, piled high with the delicious smell of stewed wild meat and ground provisions. Then in answer to the query of where he is going, he throws over his shoulder, that he is going to find a quiet place to sit and *full the big hole beneath his nose*. He abruptly stops dead in his tracks and with his free hand on his waist, collapses in laughter at his own joke. The plate of food succumbing to the jokes and tremors that his laughter produce lands on the ground, much to the gratification of the two hungry mongrels growling and baring their teeth. The young men under the tents are howling their heads off, with one remarking amidst his fits of laughter, that they did not have to pay no seventy-five cents to go to the cinema that weekend – the cinema show, a comedy, had come to them, starring Elvin and his two hungry *pot hound dogs*.

Gold Teeth watches in disbelief as Elvin with his both hands freed now, places them on the hips of his rope waisted pants, for that's how his beltless pants are being held up, with a thin length of rope. He throws back his head and roars with laughter as he heads back to the tent for another plate of food.

Gold Teeth shudders and shuts his eyes tightly, he's thinking about his friend atop the waterfall, looking down and laughing at him, the coward, who would not leave the second tier of the rock if he ever made it there, to come up to meet him, Joseph Celestine.

Gold Teeth now tired, has decided that he won't be playing his friend's game anymore. The memories he would treasure, but not for one moment, he would attempt to go back as he has been trying to do since returning to the village. He opens his eyes just in time to see Elvin's friend Carter across the yard, adjusting the noticeably red cap on his head, given to him by Tallest. He places the cap lightly to the front of his head, atop his high *muff*, that tuft of hair above the forehead that he and every teenage boy was proudly growing and grooming, the latest hairstyle, the fad that was sweeping the village.

Carter, carefully contemplates his trek across the yard to stand beside Gold Teeth and his two friends, the *men*, in the crowd, the *'sawatees'*, the big shots, they visiting the village, only because of their best friend's death. He Carter, would love to flee the village with the men for the fast life of the city. Carter is dressed in his new continental pants, its seams *cutting*. He digs his hands in the back pockets, just like he would see them do, the saga boys in the more modernize villages or even those in the city streets to which he would peruse on a Saturday morning, to see the new trends. He, always being the first young man in the village to attempt anything *hip* that was being done in the city, whether it was in attitude, lingo or dress.

His starched and ironed cotton shirt, its color raised high, is protected by a handkerchief against the heavy Vaseline he had *plastered* in his hair. The tail of his shirt, had no chance of escaping his pants, it being held down by the brand new leather belt around his narrow waist – one of the many gifts sent to him by his beloved *nenny*, one of his two godmothers from Brooklyn New York. Carter nervously shoves off with the new walk-in *style* but not executed smoothly. With his head hung low, really low and tilted to the side, hands still dug into his pockets, Carter begins to do the *Bump*. Most eyes are on Carter – his friends, admiringly so. One or two of the *force ripe young men*, those always acting older than their years, instinctively reaches up to their heads pretending to scratch their foreheads, just in case an elder was casting a scrutinizing eye. In reality, the *youth men* were reaching up to feel if their muffs were ready to make an appearance – just like Carter their Idol had often done; he teasing them about their *ingrowing hair*. Ironically, where Carter is concerned the old saying rings true, *'Monkey doh see he own tail!'*

Carter's friends and the youngsters keep looking at him admiringly, grudgingly even, wishing that they too had the charisma, to execute the slickness and confidence that he has in his walk. They having all grown up playing their favorite sports; Cricket and football, getting the same results, whether their bats were fashioned from coconut branches, from finished wood or any such thing lying around the yard and their balls, whether bought in a store out of the village or a *'young'* orange or grapefruit. Yet, there was something about Carter that stood out; He had that *'special something!'*

Carter's eyes are glued to the three men; desperately hoping that he is making a good impression, showing that he is of city material. After all, weren't they once from the village also? He is hoping to impress Gold Teeth in particular – his maybe ticket to a better life. He's fed up with the village, his friends, Elvin in particular, with his stale jokes and his penchant for ***bussing*** a fatigue or two, on anyone at inappropriate times.

Oftentimes, when talking to his Ma about his frustrations, Carter would have to concede that he was *'not catching his nennen,'* having a hard time. He, like everyone in the village, had enough to eat and though having to sometimes wear patched and darned clothing, they were always clean and that definitely bore no part of his frustrations – he just was not satisfied with ***village life***.

Now, the youth man Carter is uncomfortably aware that inquiring eyes are upon him. He begins to sweat, the beads of perspiration running down from his head into his eyes, on to his lips, tickling them into uncomfortable twitches. He is getting closer to the three men – his rescuers? Getting ever so close to his Idol, Gold Teeth.

His hands! He does not know what to do with the hands now out of his pockets. Something is going embarrassingly wrong! His feet, they are becoming entangled with each other. His walk, the crawl, the bump, it is going all wrong! Was it step, bump, step or bump, bump step? To crown it all, he trips over a small stone. From the now stubbed toe, he feels the pain coursing through every nerve and sinew of his body. He looks down at his previously white watchicong which he had scrubbed and put out on the stone bleach to dry. He looks down again at his footwear, the front of the left side now bright red with the blood of his busted big toe.

Gold Teeth Looks up into the night sky; *"Help me!"* He demands through gritted teeth. He then turns toward his friends Big Ches' and Tallest. Chewing slowly on the matchstick between his teeth, he is deep in thought. This time, not about the going ons in the village but on his successful gambling clubs in the city.

Gold Teeth catches Carter's eyes and motions with his hands, that he should slow down. He cannot tell if the pain in the young man's eyes is caused by his many, many stumbles in trying to prove himself through his still very young life or his now stubbed toe, he having seen Carter's embarrassing encounter with the stone.

Gold Teeth standing between his two friends rests his hand on their shoulders and begins nudging them out of the crowd – they understand just what his actions mean, as they head to the conspicuously shiny red car – Elvin and his friends handiwork for which they earned more money than they expected.

Yes, they know and accept that Gold Teeth is not staying for Pa Joe Joe's funeral – he has had enough, Carter disturbs him, troubles his soul – his wounds have reopened once again; are raw and oh so painful – he is bleeding badly, Gold Teeth.

He is seeing so much of himself in Carter's eyes. He does not wish to relive the past; His short stint in prison soon after arriving in the city. He too, was just once the village boy, trying too hard and fast to prove himself. He slips behind the steering wheel and slams the door, his friends doing the same, slipping into their seats and slamming their doors.

Pretending to be adjusting the rearview mirror, Gold Teeth sneaks a look at Carter, who is standing at the side of the track, looking after the car in disbelief – his hopes cruelly dashed.

Gold Teeth looks up into the night sky – it is clear. Not a cloud nor even a twinkling star has put in an appearance for him, for the last time. *He* does not appear either. Quickly he tosses another look in the rearview mirror before he drives off – Carter is standing in the middle of the dirt track, the stingy brimmed hat is now off his head and being held against his chest, against his racing heart, Gold Teeth surmises. Gold Teeth looks up to the sky again – why was he doing this, still hoping? He should know that he would not appear, ever again. It was over, that time of their life, a very long time ago.

Ma Jo Jo, on seeing the car slowly drive away, releases the black drape from which she was hiding behind all this time and eventually closes the door on another chapter of her life. Tomorrow she will be burying her husband.

Chapter 12

Alarmed, Ma Jo Jo keeps on looking at the clock on her bureau – its two am. She had been ruminating back and forth on her past, for over nine hours now! Ma Jo Jo takes another sip at her cup of **bush tea**, her fifth cup, only this time it's not her favorite *'lime bud'* but the practical **'soursop'**, which is doing its job of calming her, as the many do attest to the power of its leaves.

With her forehead pressed against the wooden walls of her bedroom, Ma Jo Jo squints and bats her lashes against the forceful breeze and rain sprinkles that's coming through the cracks of the wooden walls. She is hearing the items outside, that may not have been secured or bolted down, being tossed around by the violent winds. Her eyes are now focused on the little house higher up the hill, Ma Z's. With her fingers tightly crossed behind her back she breathes out cautiously and whispers, *'so far so good'*, on seeing the lamplight flickering in the old woman's drawing room, through the wider cracks of the wooden walls.

Ma Jo Jo makes a double sigh which is full of regret for the life that she and the old woman have lived. She makes a solemn promise to make amends after the storm; To make the first gesture of friendship and without even mentioning Pa Joe Joe, who the old woman blames for their chaotic, miserable lives. Ma Jo Jo knows differently though, it was all on her; every destroyed life. She sighs remorsefully, reaches for the enamel cup and drains it, swallowing those last drops in one big gulp.

On her way to the kitchen with the cup in hand, Ma Jo Jo stops dead in her tracks. She's hearing the offkey singing voice. Her cackling sounding laughter, resounding over the pouring rain and rolling thunder. Ma Z is definitely at it again, what she started the very night after Pa Joe Joe's funeral – the very day that he was put in the ground.

Ma Jo Jo was put off by her behavior that night and even now, wishes that she would immediately put an end to it. She had heard from Elvin's Ma, that the neighbors thought that Ma Z was being disrespectful, gleeful even of his death and was *'throwing words'* through the songs she was performing. Yes, performing, since what she was doing, definitely could not be considered, just singing!

Ma Jo Jo shakes her head in annoyance, for the misguided and malicious thoughts of her neighbors. This ***slight*** though determined old woman, throwing words and ugly words at that, to an unhearing Pa Joe Joe, was utter nonsense! They should know that she would not shy away from speaking her mind to anyone's face good or bad – ***throwing words my foot*** Ma Jo Jo thinks annoyed. Ma Z had taken on the whole village over forty years ago, confronted anyone who would ***mauvais langue*** her Josephine – *that* she did not let anyone get away with; oh no! Not bad talk her sweet Josephine!

Now Ma Jo Jo doubles back to the bedroom, her face pressed against the board window peering through its cracks and wondering about Ma Z and what her thoughts might be on this, a most scary night.

~~~

Ma Z had heard enough talk about this storm or hurricane that was now battering her neighborhood, as if determined to obliterate it before leaving. Besides making adequate the preparations for this *monster*, Ma Z was happy that it gave her the chance at seeing after yet another important factor: giving the Young One the key to an important component of her life.

With a hand playing with the two scraggly hairs on her chin, her mind is still on the so-called weather experts on the radio as they railed on and on about the mileage of the winds that determine its power or title at that given moment. Ma Z shook her head
~~~

dismissively and grunted: *'those expots'* as she tuned out the weather experts on the radio.

She checked out the barrel in the far corner of the kitchen, it was full to the brim with drinking water. She shook her head thoughtfully, still puzzled by this oncoming storm – a strange phenomenon in the middle of the dry season.

The barrel with the water to wash her wares, sat on the outside beneath her kitchen window, seated on a platform of bricks and a sheet of ply board. Her eyes rested on the brightly plastic covered tabletop, puzzling at the up turned plastic at one end. Bending low, Ma Z saw the previously held cooking oil tins now scrubbed clean and full with drinking water. Going closer and bending even lower, Ma Z wondered why a **bull pistle**, that dangerous weapon, was placed atop the metal sheeting covering the three tins.

Did she anticipate having to **buss** some lashes with the bull pistle on someone who might be *'chupid'* enough, yes, so foolhardy to come in and try to steal her water during or after the storm? After the storm, the reliable sources of water, the streams, ponds and rivers most certainly would be ravaged and polluted.

Ma Z looked protectively at the tins she had paid seventy-five cents **a piece** for and smiled thinly on remembering the back and forth she had with the shop owner before settling on the seventy-five cents for each tin. Then, she made sure that he had seen her eye rolls of disbelief and displeasure.

As she exited the store, tripping over the tins, she breathed a sigh of relief, saying under her breath **'I know from where my help comes from'**. This she said on seeing the forlorn looking Elvin **liming** by himself, a first for him, hanging out alone, **propping up** the walls of the Chineseman's shop. Ma Z made a silly joke, calling him *Samson* and reassuring him that the walls of the shop would not fall if he was to move away; He offered a pathetic smile.

Ma Z was about to ask his help in taking the tins to her home up the hill, when he quickly offered. She was hoping too, that he would see the Young One, with whom he was just now forging a relationship, she having **done**, broken up, with the one on the **putt**

putt machine, the shirt jac, sandals wearing, big haired, uppity one from the city. She just then realized that she did not know his name, never wanting too anyway.

Ma Z let loose with all the derisive descriptions on him she had ever heard; He breaking her little one's heart. She made a halfhearted attempt at making the sign of the cross, now that it was all over between them, but then decided against it, she not a believer in signing herself, not even in prayer. Then she gritted her teeth – the Young One **was** going to America, this she was going to make happen!

Ma Z felt a rush of guilt; she shouldn't ever be a participant to anyone's heartbreak again! She knew that *he* who was outside, down on his knees, vigorously scrubbing away at the oil in the tins with a bit of fiber, gravel and blue soap; In reality was scrubbing at the anger and the feeling of desolation that was about to come. Anyway, what was it with the young women of the village? Yes, all of them, if given the chance, to up and leave to *this America?*

On the completion of his ridding the tins of all it's unwanted residue, he tacked onto them, make shifts handles from bits of wood, then filled them with water from one of the full barrels in the yard and placed them beneath Ma Z's kitchen table.

After handing over the two dollars to Elvin which he reluctantly accepted, Ma Z walked over to her bedroom that she had long given up to the Young One, with much protestations from her and she, sleeping on the cot which she opens up every night in her drawing room. Now, soon the bedroom was going to be her's once again with the Young One going to the **'States'**, United States of America, she corrected herself sharply, aware that she too had adopted the new way of addressing the great country.

Ma Z felt a sudden twinge of pain in her back and looked across at the cot standing innocently in the corner, where it usually stood in the day. Ma Z was aware that the uncomfortable cot was the source of her pain. She knew that if the Young One was not going to America, the cot was where she was destined to lie **until cock get teeth**, forever!

With tears blotting her eyes, and as if needing support, she tightly clutched at the tapestry hanging over her door. She looked at the tousled bedding – she didn't need to see this, to know that the Young One had a restless night. She was kept awake by her little moans and fitful cries during her sleep.

Ma Z was concerned, wanting to awaken the Young One from whatever dreams were disturbing her but she kept her peace – she let the Young One be. She had paid too high a price in the past, for her meddling, blamed for destroying lives. Truth be told, Ma Z had unwittingly done it yet again, she was guilty, guilty, guilty!

After Pa Joe Joe's death, Ma Z had decided that it was time to start anew – she decided to start with the Young One by unearthing the hidden past, that shaped her life, that started over forty years ago, that she was aware that the Young One knew bits and pieces of.

The Young One wept bitterly as Ma Z dug deeper and deeper. Then she stopped abruptly and stopped her narrative, she could no longer speak those horrific words, especially the horror of the life of the one living secretly in the sanatorium.

Looking into the accusatory eyes of the Young One, Ma Z shrugged her shoulders and walked to the front of the bed on which she was sitting, absorbing the news that would forever impact her – the life changing news.

Ma Z lifted the fiber mattress high – reached deep under it and carefully extracted what was once a lily-white pillowcase now discolored by age and neglect. Ma Z with trembling fingers, took out the yellowed newspaper. In fact, she saved just its cover, the first and second pages of that day's newspaper, that told the story of what she was most interested in; what was to be of their lives henceforth, even of those not yet born.

Without a glance at the Young One and bearing the vestige of self-indulgent pity, begging to be forgiven and understood, Ma Z handed her the pages of her past, her future and walked out of the room.

Ma Z could do nothing for the Young One as she pored over the article and shook with heartrending tears. Ma Z began doubting herself, should she have shown her the long-buried newspaper? Taken her to the psychiatrist, ***that one*** in the first place, when she started to show signs of her disturbing psychological issues?

The psychiatrist pulled Ma Z aside after the first visit, advising her that the Young One would be better served if she would understand her past, of which *he* is an integral part.

Looking after them, as they left his office, he felt a surge of envy, anger even, but then quickly, he put a damper on those unwanted emotions. At a young age he had decided not to take a side. After all the pain and confusion caused by his doings, '*the man*' still happened to be his father and a good one too. To top it all, the woman who was falling apart needed him and had become totally dependent on him, her young son. Regretted any of it? Did he ever had the time to contemplate or process his feelings? He was twelve years old when it happened and ever since, he had his hands full with her, his mother.

Ma Z kept on taking advantage of the billowing drapes covering the doorway, peeping in at the Young One, whose beginning was being revealed through the yellowed front page and fading ink of the newspaper in her hands. As she kept on looking in at the Young One, Ma Z began questioning herself again; should she have listened to him; the psychiatrist that the Young One's healing was wrapped up in the past? Ma Z breathed in deeply, there were just too many dark secrets. The Young One had to understand the Older One's absence, her reticence in getting close to her.

Ma Z herself, began drowning in her yesterday's – she could almost hear the gut-wrenching screams of the woman standing on the courthouse steps. See her clawing at the air for the figure now far beyond her reach, never again to be in her life – to be hers. his heart meant for someone else, who in turn would never be his. Ma Z never forgot the surprise and bewildered look on the face of the twelve-year-old boy – the now grown psychiatrist as he tugged at the screaming woman. That was the beginning of the rest of his life – always looking after his mother.

Ma Z sighed, there indeed were traces of silver linings in bringing the past to light. The psychiatrist informed, that he too had begun delving into the past with his mother, showing her pictures of those she might be receptive to meeting. Then on hearing about and seeing pictures of the Young One, the woman acquiesced to a meeting with her but on hearing that the woman was now referring to her as her *granddaughter*, Ma Z noticeably flinched.

All's well that ends well on that front, Ma Z conceded, as her train of thought chugged over to the Young One and the heated argument she overheard her having with the ***motorbike boy***. Yet another nickname Ma Z had conferred on the young man, whose name she didn't wish to know, much to the Young One's chagrin.

Ma Z thought the ***'motorbike boy'*** impetuous and rude, bearing the typical persona of the town and city people. Who needed his halfhearted ***good evening*** or '***night***', accompanied by his bland stare? ***Like a zombie***, Ma Z added contemptuously to her thoughts of him and was happy when he roared away in the dark night on his noise making machine – never to come by again.

Ma Z, for the first time had hesitated and reminded herself that she should not meddle – let ***every pot sit on their own black bottom***. Yes, let everyone deal with their own problem.

~~~

Ma Z then opened the top half of the door and looked up as if studying the darkening skies and thought; *'dis coming storm or hurricane, whatever dey choose to call it, would surely be a big **macco** one – a massive one at dat!'* Some of the tin roofs on the animal sheds around the neighborhood had already been blown away by the heavy winds; Those she knew were the ones definitely not properly secured.

The previously humorous an animated chatter of the young men as they pounded away with hammers and nails, having turned into loud and serious arguments on which way was the better to secure the roofs. They were evidently now aware of the seriousness of the coming storm and their unpreparedness.
~~~

Ma Z herself, still frustrated about her apparent helplessness in not being able to deal with the Young One's turbulent life, barged out of the house and shouted downhill to the working young men; *"put logs, big stones, ol' pots, alyuh big heads, anything to hol' down de roofs, then shutup!"* Then, to break the stunned silence of the slack jawed young men looking up at her in awe and to bring some levity to the conversation which she knew that they would enjoy, she shouted with mock seriousness, *now take alyuh time and hurry up!* That did it, drew howls of laughter from the young men. Some holding onto their heads, others to their bellies, as they howled and screamed with laughter. Then she added with the same mock seriousness, face to match, *"then come an' fix my rickety steps!"* That of course, had two of the young men hurrying up the hill with hammer and nails in hands.

~~~

Ma Z was becoming restless, she couldn't dodge or shake the feeling that the wisp of black smoke encircling the bottled neck zabocca tree, was conveying a message of doom to add to the coming storm. That something of a catastrophic nature was about to descend on her neighborhood and maybe extensively throughout the whole village.

The air had become hot and stifling. The old woman looked ahead at the cattle as they lazily chewed on whatever little cuds they could bring to their mouths. Their white foam – like spittle refusing to leave their long tongues were being forced out from the sides of their mouths.

Ma Z knew why this was so – she looked down at the brown patches of grass beneath the hooves of the cattle. She craned her neck toward the far side of the foothills – under the shade of the mango tree, where she saw a large number of downturned galvanized and plastic buckets of which she wasn't in the least bit surprised. The young men had tried but could not source any water for the animals.

Ma Z felt guilty knowing how flush she was with water. The full barrel in the corner of the kitchen, the tins under the table and even
~~~

the full barrel under her kitchen window for washing her *wares* and clothes, if she so chose. Angrily she shook off the guilty feeling of her having so much water – for goodness sake, this was supposed to be in the middle of the dry season! Soon the village will be inundated with water; too much when the rainy season comes. She stomped her feet, in irritation as her thought trailed off.

Ma Z thought of the bundle of unwashed clothing piled high in a corner of her bedroom floor and just how much she was fed up of eating roast bake every day now – bake, morning, noon and night! Bake and saltfish buljol, bake and smoke herring; though, an occasional bake and eggs meant less usage of her precious water. Since the scarcity of water began, Ma Z determined that it was time to turn down her pots – no more cooking. She being *mingy*, very careful with her use of the water, least she ran out before the deluge that is the storm, comes gushing out of the clouds.

Things were getting quite serious, the cattle, other animals and fowls were literally dying of hunger and thirst. The men of the village had already scrambled to every known ravine, stream, *gutter* - to every and any small creak, and *'crack'*, literally every nook and cranny, to no avail. The young men, had not too long ago, dug a pit in what was once the swampland, but now parched and arid to bury yet another heifer. Dumped! Ma Z thought matter of factly, having seen the unemotional young men digging one pit after another.

She placed her hand over her eyes to block out the glare of the sun as she scanned the other side of what was once the swampland. She saw that the majority of the steel drums were uncovered and instinctively knew that those that were uncovered, held no more water for the animals.

Still, with one hand visor like over her eyes, she lifted the other and with a trembling finger counted ten covered drums. The drums gave her little comfort knowing that with about thirty head of thirsty cattle out there, those drums would soon be empty if not disbursed very stringently.

She sighed and shook her head in disbelief; About three weeks ago, the land on which these now *'marasme'*, these emaciated looking cattle stood, was considered swampland with lots of green grass on which they leisurely fed and were watered. Now the few blades of grass left standing were brown, harsh and surely tasteless even for the cattle, Ma Z was sure.

She looked on pityingly, as they would from time to time, listlessly swish their tails at the gnats and ticks, *'sucking the living daylights'*, drawing the blood from the weakened animals, who also had to contend with the pigeons now boldly landing on their backs and feasting on said gnats and ticks, while the flightless cranes did the same to their legs.

Like most of the **hill people**, days before the storm, Ma Z kept on hearing the squealing of the improvised wheels of the box carts, as if protesting being pushed on the stony ground – so many times by the mango eating young men, with the juices of now **in season** fruit running down their forearms. The young men while eating the fruit from one hand and with the other on the cart, raced each other downhill and along the tracks, with the empty tins and cans rattling murderously in the box carts – a grim reminder of the villagers present situation.

Ma Z, still reliving the days before the storm, in the fog of her mind, is hearing the *'putt, putt, putting'* sounds of the jitney that arrives precisely at eight o'clock every Saturday morning, with large blocks of ice to sell to all the villagers.

The old woman looked down at herself, clothed in her favorite sleepwear, the merino, one of the six that was once owned by the deceased husband of the Irish woman. It was quite *'holey'* now, rendered thread bare by lots of wear. She was given these, her now sleepwear of choice, on becoming one of the Irish woman's rotating servants on the death of her husband.

Her husband was quite a large and tall man when they first migrated from Ireland as a manager, then owner, of the largest cocoa and coconut estates in the village or as the villagers would declare empathetically, **in de whole island!** Anyway, the Irishman had quickly boiled down to less than half the size he used to be, he becoming a *'maga'*, *'maga'* man, quite the thin man. It was the flippant observation of many that if he continued losing weight that rapidly, he would soon *'dry up'* and disappear. Then shortly thereafter, it was being whispered that he had the dreaded disease, cancer!

Withdrawing from in front of the door, Ma Z reached back and grabbed for the house coat that she had previously tossed, aiming for one of the chairs around the dining room table but which instead landed on the fruit bowl, toppling it. She looked up at the crackling tin roof; the noise sounding as if the neighborhood kids were atop, pitching their marbles. Of course, she knew that this was only the result of the broiling early morning sun, mercilessly beating down on the ceiling-less roof. She looked around her small drawing room and saw that even her potted plants were bearing the brunt of the sun's fury, through the open board windows.

Before going downhill to join the neighbors with their assorted enamel and plastic bowls in hand for their ice, Ma Z made sure that her door was properly closed behind her. She did not need a thirsty lizard or zandouille crawling inside and finding its way in any of her containers of drinking water, as one had recently done. She had found it floating, its pale bloated underbelly and blue veins staring her in the face. Ma Z shudders in horror and scorn – she knew that if it happened again, even with the water shortage, she would not hesitate to spill it out together with the dead revolting reptile. Not one of her equally thirsty plants, would get a taste of that contaminated water, she swore. She shuddered again, before grabbing for her crocus bag and slamming her door shut.

As she neared Ma Jo Jo's house, the old woman's eyes skimmed over the still shuttered board door and windows, then to the little church in the back. She noted that it was still shuttered after two weeks of **him** being gone. *May it never ever be opened again*, she crisply wished upon the little church. Then with a **cut eye**, she quickly withdrew her eyes from the house and church; She didn't want to be **caught dead** by Ma Jo Jo **_minding her business! 'May be even now, she is maccoing through the cracks of her door or window,'_** Ma Z thought of Ma Jo Jo, who like everybody else in the village, kept abreast of a lot of the *going ons* through the cracks of their board houses.

As she scurried down the hill, Ma Z heard the iceman's shouts from atop the back of his jitney; *"Ice! Ice! Ice!"* on his having finally settled for a spot under a large shady tree. The customers in return responds, languidly, yawning and stretching, as they removed themselves from under the shade of the breadfruit and chataigne trees and ambled over to him. Some offered up their twenty-five or fifty cent pieces, others their dollar notes, not sure that the Iceman would make it to their section of the village, the next day, Sunday, when more people tended to buy the most ice.

The old woman with her dollars' worth of ice sitting in her crocus bag at the side of the track, walked to the middle and flailed her arms above her head, trying to catch the attention of any of the young men standing idly by, with their unusually large red battery-operated radio. She did not succeed and walked back to her ice in the crocus bag. Today, more than any other, she needed the help to take her ice up the hill to her home – she had bought a large chunk – the largest she had ever bought.

From the faces of the young men she could see, she did not recognize anyone, in the animatedly chattering group. The neighborhood and what she had heard through the grapevine, the whole village was changing too, full with young people who refused to say good morning or good night. She did not like this one bit – looking down at her crocus bag, she saw that water was trickling out – that meant her ice was melting – if only Elvin or one of his friends were around.

She walked back to the center of the track - rude or not, one of those young men were going to **'offer'** to take her ice up the hill to her home! Salt, to sprinkle on the ice in order to prevent its fast melt, was already sitting on the table with quite a lot of gazette paper to wrap it. Now, if she could only catch the attention of one of those young men who after taking the ice to her kitchen, she would politely ask to divide the ice for the two weekend days.

She again began to flail her arms above her head and yet again, did not succeed in attracting any of them. In frustration she began clapping her hands and at the same time calling out, '***aye dere, aye dere young men***!' Alerted by the frenetic tone in her voice, all heads quickly turned in her direction and immediately two of the young ymen started running over to her. Then, as she pointed to the crocus bag lying at the side of the track, and up the hill, one of the young men fell off, while the other continued his trot over to her.

The young man picked up the bag and followed Ma Z, who smiled guiltily and noted that maybe, they the old timers, were wrong about the young newcomers; that they were not all bad. Ma Z momentarily stopped in front of Ma Jo Jo's house. Concerned about her still shuttered door and windows, she thought of going to rouse her if she was really still asleep, or perhaps peeping at her through the cracks of her house; Ma Z decided against the former.

Before pushing ahead, Ma Z cast her eyes to the church at the back of the house and sighed heavily, deciding angrily that Ma Jo Jo was indeed a big fool for letting that *running boy* destroy her life, both their lives.

Ma Z could feel her *'blood beginning to boil, her blood pressure beginning to rasie,'* knowing that Ma Jo Jo blamed her for every single thing that did not come out the way she planned. Yes and blaming her for everything real or imagined, these past two weeks since Pa Joe Joe's passing. Was she to be blamed for his *jing toe*, his busted and neglected big toe that led to his death? With the young man and the ice in the crocus bag in tow behind her, she crossed to the other side and continued her trek up the hill to her home.

Chapter 13

Feeling utterly miserable, Ma Jo Jo creeps up on her bed, pulls her favorite flannel blanket around her shoulders and closes her eyes – she wishes that sleep would come to her, would stop evading her. She can't understand why thoughts of Ma Z is plaguing her and why tonight at this time, when the storm is predicted to hit the hardest. She wants to clear her mind of these thoughts because they always lead back to the concert and it's cumulative effects over forty years ago.

She is tossing and wondering if she should head to the kitchen for just one more cup of that sleep inducing soursop tea, that somehow won't lull her to sleep tonight. She's listening to the wind, freely whooshing through her house, tossing those folded but not yet put away light curtains that she had taken down and washed the evening after Pa Joe Joe's funeral, despite not feeling well.

On hearing about Ma Jo Jo's **state**, a few days later, Ma Z had barged into Ma Jo Jo's house, demanding that she be given chores to do, until she felt well enough. Looking around her surprisingly untidy dining room, she accused Ma Jo Jo of being depressed – why else would she, a very neat and tidy person still have those curtains sitting on her highly polished mahogany dining table, her pride and joy?

Ma Jo Jo was adamant; she did not need help, much less Ma Z's. She pushed back at Ma Z in the ugliest of ways, reminding her that she never **putfoot** in the house when Pa Joe Joe was here, never mind, that she wasn't welcomed by him, so now, she should go away and let her be!

Ma Z grumbled that Ma Jo Jo was being **harden**, stubborn, just like an old donkey. Her eyes twinkled as she shook with silent laughter, as she equated Ma Jo Jo with Elvin's old donkey. Then, as she stormed back up the hill to her house, she warned Ma Jo Jo that she might not be around if she was to **kilkitay**, fall over. Ma Jo Jo looked after the bent old woman as she slowly climbed up the hill and wondered why was there this fierce tugging of her heart strings?

~~~

With the next gust of wind through her house, Ma Jo Jo hears the toppling of some of the filled plastic drinking cups on her mahogany table and therefore on her just washed curtains too. She does not hear the thunder rolls and is not startled by the sudden burst of orange and blue hues of the lightning, silently and quickly zigzagging its way in and out of her bedroom.

The storm raging for close to ten hours now, has Ma Jo Jo nonplussed but nonetheless grateful that her tin roof is holding up. She gathers up the coverlet, most of it having fallen off the bed, then carefully tucks it under her body, her face remaining exposed. She sighs blissfully – the soursop tea while not lulling her off to sleep, has taken off the **edge** and calmed her a great deal.

She's hearing the plop plop of the raindrops running off the carpenter nails, those nails with the largest of heads, pounding into the roof and now being used as a run-off for the rain into the containers, that she had the good sense to place indiscriminately over the drawing room floor - the leaks seemingly all over the roof.

The very distinctive plop plopping sounds, she knows are the droplets that are now falling on her mahogany dining table and wagonette; She worries, that just mere hours ago she had taken so much time, on those two prized pieces of furniture; buffing and shining them with her special rags and ocedar polish.

Emotional tears, now blurring her vision in the flickering candle lit room, causes Ma Jo Jo to draw the flannel blanket tighter around her; A gift from the Older One in the *States* – given to her four years ago for Mother's Day but **a week after the big day** and again, *through* Ma Z.
~~~

Ma Jo Jo cannot fathom why she chose to use the coverlet on a miserable and uncertain day like today but it sure is feeling good, comforting even – like big warm arms hugging her closely; Pa Joe Joe's maybe? She shuts her eyes tightly against the images her mind is creating, wishing for.

In the midst of her merciful and blissful fog, Ma Jo Jo is listening to the angry voices of Ma Z and the Older One ...They are way, way back in the past. Ma Z is *'bouffing'* the Older One, scolding her, telling her to stop with her *'womanish ways'* and to march down the hill with the wildflowers that she had roused the *'harden'* child from her bed to go pick from the fields and present to Ma Jo Jo on this special day – Mother's Day.

Now Ma Jo Jo is groaning in pain, she is inflicted with searing emotional pain, now that her fog is lifted and there is no place to hide, or no disguise to use. It's all coming to her now with brute force, on finally accepting the fact that like the wildflowers, the blanket was also a forced gift.

Th Older One being already here one week, for Mother's Day, had presented her gift of the blanket after the event had already passed. Maybe it was not even meant for her but was forced out of her by Ma Z – Yet another one, a forced gift Ma Jo Jo assumes.

Enraged, Ma Jo Jo tosses aside the coverlet, and is suddenly startled by the sound of something slamming into her door. She puzzles at what the object might be but soon gives up. On a night like this, there will likely be countless more items slamming not only into her doors, but her windows, roof, the whole *blame* house!

Her eyes sweeping over the room, rests on the framed picture on the bureau; a picture of the young Joseph Celestine. She sits upright, her bare feet firmly planted on the soaked and sodden flooring boards due to the rainwater slowly trickling down the sides of the walls. With her hands firmly on her thighs as if for support, least she falls face down on the water-soaked floor, she peers into the photograph that reminds her of the time her life was suddenly upended.

Ma Jo Jo quietly shakes her head at it and wonders; *'why couldn't he understand?'* looking deep into the photograph as if seeing it for the first time and slowly coming to the realization that the last forty years were wasted years – not worth it. Reaching over for the photograph, she snorts, *'dis farce is going to end right here, right now!'* and swings around, smashing the photograph against the bed head. The bed on which they laid on every night but never really shared.

Ma Jo Jo looks at the shards of glass on the bed; a shard having completely sheared the head off the body of the photograph, yet still remaining in the shattered frame. The droplets of blood from her hand, pierced by a piece of broken glass and now dropping on the sheared off neck, seems bone chilling enough, to have Ma Jo Jo shuddering.

She keeps on looking at the photograph that was taken upon his release from prison. Pa Joe Joe Insisted that it must be framed and kept on the bureau. In the beginning, Ma Jo Jo could not bear the knife life stabs of pain to her heart she experienced whenever her eyes fell on the photograph; *her punishment*, sitting right in front her face.

~~~

Ma Jo Jo examines the broken skin on her hand and emotionlessly plucks the tiny splinters from the swollen hand. She nonchalantly raises an eyebrow as yet another violent crushing sound of thunder and explosive lightning invade her space.

Now, only because of something crashing down on her roof, shaking her house violently as if wanting to shake it off it's *'pillar trees,'* it's columns; that Ma Jo Jo looks up, only to see that this violent turbulence has forced her window open. She runs to the window that is being repeatedly slammed against the wall by the raging winds and holds onto it.

Instinctively, she knows that the earth-shattering sound on the roof has come from one of her trees, felled by the raging winds. Suddenly, her tussle with the window has come to an end – it's over. She reluctantly concedes that she has lost the war and is about to hand over the prize, the window, when it is ripped from her hand
~~~

and is slammed for the last time against the wall, hanging by only one hinge.

Aghast, Ma Jo Jo stares into the dark night, it's total blackness and gives a brittle but determined laugh — she would not be intimidated by it. This was her life for over forty years — blackness! She reveled in it.

Ma Jo Jo grimaces and clinches both her fists and teeth tightly. She must not think about the Young One at a time like this, least the Older One comes into her consciousness too — this she must avoid at all costs, so she goes to her favorite means of escape, singing one of her favorite songs, doing so louder and louder.

Through the swaying branches, Ma Jo Jo can see by the lights of the dark moon, the steady rain falling like steel spears, piercing the earth. Despite the rain lashing at her through the now windowless frame, she is determined to keep her position there — she is keeping a keen eye on the little house higher up the hill.

The busted fruit, the yellow buttery flesh scattered all over the ground, confirm her suspicions, that it was indeed one of her avocado trees that was felled by the storm.

Ma Jo Jo squints as she peers again with concern into the darkness towards the hill, from where she can hear the water gushing down and also from the light that shines through the branches of the trees, she can discern most of the items as they tumble along by the water to the bottom of the hill. She realizes that some of the items have come from Ma Z's unfinished gallery; the pair of cane bottomed rocking chairs that Ma Z was so proud of receiving — yet another gift from the Older One, on one of her visits back from the *states*. Once, after Ma Z quickly intimated that Ma Jo Jo could have those chairs on her passing, did Ma Jo Jo realize that the emotional pain of her not having a relationship with the Older One might have manifested itself on her face.

Ma Jo Jo sighs, wishing that the storm and all that it brought along with it would end already. She looks at the clock on the bureau — it had stopped its tick tocking, the day that Pa Joe Joe died, but she just could not deal with it; rewinding it, knowing its history. She feels the tears trickling down her cheeks. She does not try to check them as she laughingly breaks into another song; *My grandfather's clock was too high for the shelf* ...Ma Jo Jo stops suddenly, she looks at the clock with contempt and sneers, *an unnecessary item*! Like most in the village, she knew when it was five in the morning through the crowing of the rooster atop the pig pen, or by the two that would curiously sleep in the tallest of her banana plants. Then, she would know that it was seven in the morning after hearing the blowing of the horn in the cocoa estate, alerting the workers to the start of their workday. Again, any fool could '*guestimate*' the time in between or go outside and the shadow of the sun seen on the ground would '*accurately*' tell the time.

Now, the marooned Ma Jo Jo, like most in the houses standing on '*pillar trees*' is coming to the realization of the calamitous position she's in. The water lapping at the top of the '*pillar trees*' is coming through the cracks of her flooring boards.

Ma Jo Jo listlessly gets off the bed and moves to the drawing room where she decides that it will be less stressful looking through the cracks in the door at the events playing out, in the yard. She sees the dead chickens, ducks and mangy dog, whose ribs seems to be threatening to bust through its hairless and thin skin. The ram-goat too, its horn embedded in a small fallen tree as it floats by; she thinks that she sees some limp movements of its tail and makes to go and rescue it, only to realize that it too, is dead. She establishes this through the oil drum that floats by, '*soundly*' knocking the animal without any reaction from it.

Ma Jo Jo Is looking emotionlessly at the destruction that the vast watery grave is flaunting in her face. Suddenly, the water is volatile in its movements, angrily so. Ma Jo Jo shifts from foot to foot and awaits to see the fool or animal, wading through such treacherous even though shallow waters, what with all sorts of dangers lurking underfoot. Really, what living fool or animal would take *God out of their thoughts* to venture out before '*day clean*', even before the break of dawn and on a day such as this? She rhetorically asks herself – her face pressed even closer on the door as if that would ensure a better view.

It's the Young One! Ma Jo Jo has come alive, her frenetic motions have been kickstarted, she is moving from the board windows to the board door. Her movements, alike a '*setting*' hen, who has been disturbed from her nest. The Young One is now in deep waters, the waters swirling around her and pushing her in the direction of the river to which she is heading anyway.

Ma Jo Jo wants to call out to her and warn her about the overflowing and now treacherous river but knows that her words would have no effect on her – not even if she gets out and physically tries to hold her; succeeding in stopping her for a while. This is her time, the darkness, the ugliness. Is this really her time for revelry too? Ma Jo Jo wonders.

Ma Jo Jo removes herself from the cracks, the peepholes, the lies, the deceit – she is tired of viewing the world through those prisms. She breathes out, thankful that she did stay in and the Young One did not *lock eyes* with her, or her eyes falling on her guilty face. It was too soon, since the Young One learned her truth from Ma Z and the psychiatrist. She quickly whispers a hopeful prayer that the man of the bushes is there, somewhere near the river as he always is, to protect her, if need be.

As if from a sign from above, Ma Jo Jo hears the crowing of a rooster and with that, she once again moves from the drawing room to the now windowless bedroom. Ma Jo Jo is looking at Ma Z's empty shopping basket as it careens with a heap of sand and silt. She frowns at the sight of the basket now bereft of all its ground provisions, the root vegetables, that she surely must have bought yesterday, her usual Saturday market day.

Ma Jo Jo is reduced to uncontrollable giggles as Ma Z's flaked and dented enamel '*posey*', her bright blue chamber pot, comes into view, she wonders if the old woman was sitting on it, as it was swept away.

Ma Jo Jo looks on in amazement as the window that was hanging on its lone hinge frees itself and goes flying into the semidarkness. Above her, two sheets of her galvanize roofing have been ripped off and like the window, they too have taken flight to somewhere in the bushes.

Ma Jo Jo casts her eyes higher up the hill and becomes aware that something is awry with the little house up there; She blinks and blinks again. Ma Z's house, or part of it is not there anymore! It has collapsed but hopefully not on her. The ***pillar trees***, those sturdy wooden columns made from the trees, cut right there in the village's forest, are still standing – standing sure and strong like Ma Z once did.

Ma Jo Jo sees the thin waft of white smoke arising amidst the collapsed house. Despite what she has just seen through the window, she moves away and sits on the bed as if in shock or some sort of stupor. Maybe the smoke is signaling that everything is alright with the old woman? If not, another regret in life she knows that she won't be able to withstand.

She puzzles at the destroyed framed photograph at her feet, wondering how it got there. Quickly, she bends and picks up the two sheared pieces of the photo and deftly begins to put them together again in the shattered frame. Ma Jo Jo looks proudly at her handiwork, despite the pain of her swollen finger that still has some splinters embedded therein.

Just as quickly, she gets off the bed and leans the damaged frame against her bed head, tracing the outline of his face with the blood that's seeping from the tip of her fore finger, but now the sharp stinging in the palm of her hand also, is forcing her to desist. She takes this as a sign that '*he*' is talking to her, no, scolding her yet again; ***yuh ded to me, you got to leave me, now! Now! Now!***

Those words that he screamed at her more in pain than anger, now keeps reverberating around the room, escaping through the roof now short of two galvanize sheets of roofing, and through the windowless rooms, soaring maybe up to the roaring waterfall; Where now he would surely receive his spitefully said words with satisfaction, before sending them back to torment her over and over.

Ma Jo Jo is back to it again ... If he was here, Pa Joe Joe, he would be out there in the rain, hammer and nails in hand repairing her broken steps and whatever else was broken. His sleeveless merino drenched with rain and sweat, sticking to his muscular body. The dungaree pants, the one with the big loops, the extraordinarily large loops to accommodate the equally large brass buckle, the belt that he bought since ...Ma Jo Jo begins to descend into the hell of her own making. Now, why did she go there, knowing exactly what and where the clothing represent. Not the belt though, the belt was added after he had obtained his freedom.

Often times when riding on the bus, she would see them, the gangs dressed alike, chopping away at the huge logs at the edge of the forest. Her heart would be doing flip flops on seeing her *Joseph Celestine's* baleful eyes, looking after the passing bus and not being able to catch a glimpse of his *Josephine'*, who all this time would be sitting low in her seat, hiding; Hiding the fact that she had her freedom and he, not his, all because of her.

~~~

Before leaving to go up to Ma Z, Ma Jo Jo cast her eyes on the photograph leaning against the bed head, but she does not see him – she would love to blame the blinding tears for this, but she has slowly come to the realization that she had not really '*seen*' him nor known him for the past forty years, even though they were under the same roof.

She looks at the water soundlessly rocking her rickety steps, gently rocking them to and fro as if to an inaudible lullaby. Carefully she descends what's left of the steps, mindful that three steps are not there anymore, swept away by the floodwaters.

Ma Jo Jo is carefully and laboriously wading her way through the surprising amount of garbage floating downhill. She is sweating profusely because of what have just '*passed*' her and the rest of the villagers; She looks up at the semi darkened sky. Thankfully, the rain is not **'peltin down'** anymore. She notes that the fowls of the air and earth are not yet foraging about for sustenance; A lot they would get on a morning like this.

Ma Jo Jo often losing her footing, slipping and sliding, has decided to go down on all fours as she makes her way up hill. Surprised at the sudden gush of water sweeping over her, Ma Jo Jo looks up and Pa Joe Joe is standing there, a giant force against the tumultuous waters leaping up to his strong broad shoulders, angrily pushing and lashing at him, wanting him to get out of the way – The waters, they really wanting to get at Ma Jo Jo. She reaches up
~~~

and extends her arm to Pa Joe Joe but he does not take it – he isn't here, never was.

She struggles up and breathes deeply; looking down at the rot left on the muddied hill, the water having quickly dissipated into the porous ground, or run off over the side of the hill, into the precipice below.

Ma Jo Jo grits her teeth with determination, swearing that from now on her footing will be sure and steady, in every aspect of her life. Now, bogged down by her soaked and muddied clothing, she slavishly pulls herself up hill. She begins to sing, then; Pa Joe Joe ... **_Must not go there_**, she chides herself. She redirects her thoughts, to yet another song, this time, one from her childhood, when life was not so entangled, so complicated.

Pa Joe Joe's image refuses to go away from her. Ma Jo Jo's voice is becoming shriller and shriller. Out of nowhere, comes this old stool seat, it leaving the loose clump of hill that it was stuck on, suddenly breaking free and sliding into her. The further she gets up hill, the further she goes into her childhood, her youth.

Mr. Leo is looking on approvingly at his would-be singing star! She sees him and is not afraid of him anymore, just wary. She does not change the tone of her shrill voice. Her voice that is now rending the air, causing the sky to rain down blood. Her voice is shaking the earth – the trees are creaking and weeping.

Pa Joe Joe is angry and uncontrollable, caught up in the fight between the thunder and lightning yet still going after Mr. Leo. Finally, winded but hopeful, Ma Jo Jo pauses and looks up to Pa Joe Joe for his approval; She does not get it. Again, he is not here, never was.

~~~

For some strange reason, the winds down in the valley are at their riotous best today. The winds bellowing threateningly, bending, twisting and even uprooting some of the trees, have now caused the few birds that had stayed behind to watch over their just hatched young, to take flight.
~~~

The trees are weeping because she is leaving them. They have to stop her; She belongs to them, to the river. For all those years she has belonged to them, been family. Even the corbeaus, those filth loving angry birds, circling above, are bent on stopping her. The incessant shrill noises being heard throughout, are the voices of the angry forest coming together, they are bent on stopping her; they all must stop her.

First to ever try taking her away, were the rudderless young people, with their nestlike hairstyles and new mode of dressing, who would gather daily in the city square, mouthing off their idealism, their newfound doctrines. Then came the Older Ones from abroad, with their fancy way of talking, wanting to take her away, far, far, away from them, in a *'flying bird'* an aeroplane! Take her away from the trees, the waterfall, the river, the fishes, the crabs and even the crapauds with their nonsensical noises. Take her away from the man in the bushes too, to a place of concrete, glass and steel, a place so raw, harsh and cold!

The Young One, sitting on the bank of the river, with the violent winds whipping at her and the water rushing over her dangling legs, is broken. For the very first time since making his promise to her, Pa Joe Joe has broken it. Didn't he promise to be there whenever she called on him? Then, call on him she will!

The forest is filling up with her soulful, frenetic voice, shouting out his name, pleading with him to come and save her. Now, above the noise of the tumultuous waters rushing down the hill into the overflowing river; she hears it; the eerie silence. She sees him now, way above all the muck and debris of the river. Above the bent and broken bamboos, bopping up and down in the river, as the water gushes over them, their roots refusing to leave their stool ... Their birthplace.

Two gigantic immortelle trees are forced from their home high above the waterfall, their roots loosened from deep within the earth, after maybe hundreds of years. With most of their crimson flowers intact, they have landed just beneath the waterfall, it's furiously flowing waters barely nudging their massive trunks. And here is Pa Joe Joe floating above this all.

The Young One is choking on her sobs. Why did she even for a moment, question his promise to be always here for her? Her heart is racing just as fast as her quickening footsteps – not even thinking of what might be lying beneath them. Her eyes never blinking, she, keeping them laser focused on him, the painfully thin man.

But wait, Pa Joe Joe was never a thin man and why is he dressed in a frock made of crocus bags? She stops and stares at the figure that is now morphing into the man of the bushes; she's confused. She lifts a hand to her throbbing forehead. Oh! She thought that it was all over ...the on and off fever.

Before leaving her house for the last time, the old woman had explained to her, that her '***seeing things***', her hallucinations, were brought on by the very high fever and forbade her to get out of bed without her knowing. She was too weak to fight with the old woman, otherwise she would have told her to stay out of her life just as the others had certainly told her, in the past.

She had never seen the man of the bushes near the waterfall but often on the huge rock in the middle of the river. She lifts her head and sees his encouraging smile, his sympathetic eyes. Maybe he would have the answer to the multitude of questions waiting to tumble out of her troubled soul. Alas, it seems too late; the words keep churning up inside, rising up to the point of choking her but refusing to come out.

She hears herself screaming out in deafening silence, "*it matters nothing to me that the village celebrates my so-called successes when I don't even know who I am. I'm emotionally broken. I want me, I need me, please, help me find myself!*" She silently flings those gut-wrenching pleas to him, the man of the bushes, who's now atop the rock, his rock. The man of the bushes crouches down, elbows on his knees, hands cupping his chin, getting comfortable in expectancy for a long discourse with her.

She wistfully smiles up at him, as if wishing that he would come down from his rock, take her in his arms and assure her that things would be alright now. She smiles wanly, knowing that their fates have already been sealed and not wanting to complicate their lives anymore, she reaches up and with the back of her hand, blots out those utterly *'silly, silly'* tears from creeping out.

So much have been said of this remarkably thin man. His strength and prowess being legendary. She smiles at the oft told tale of his rescuing a pregnant sow from certain death with his bare hands, after it fell into a cesspit.

The man of the bushes smiles back at her, his face lighting up as if turned on by some giant switch in his head. Now, the previously slow-moving waters comes rushing down the hill, straight into the river. The waterfall seeming to be in on this sudden upheaval, its waters can be heard pounding onto the rocks. The river too, seems to be in on the chaos with its waters forming into mountainous waves, tossing about everything in their wake. The waterfall having finally gotten it's way with the immortelle trees, breaking them to smithereens, seems to be coming together with the river. The broken trees crashing again and again against the rock as if trying to get to the man of the bushes, to bring him down.

The Young One does not understand this, the sudden and violent disturbances by the elements in the river. She decides to engage the man of the bushes, so she shouts out, almost pleadingly, *"don't you have something to say to me, anything?"*

The man of the bushes is back on his feet again, tears running down his cheeks. The girl turns to walk away; She kicks viciously then stomps on the head of the snake that unfortunately crosses path with her today; A dangerous mappire at that. The man of the bushes giggles, thinking that the Older One would have done just that … kicked the dangerous snake without batting an eyelid too!

Before taking leave of him and the village, she bends down and with one hand, scoops up some water with which she quickly blesses herself. She luxuriously inhales what she'll be leaving behind. The clean forest air and every other scent that comes with it. Then there's the river that meant everything to Pa Joe Joe and herself.

She throws her eyes toward the hill but through the tangle of fallen trees and lots of their broken limbs, she cannot now see the little house that she had left in anger, amidst the shocking revelation of her creation. She feels herself growing cold and tense and knows from where this is coming from. She curses at Ma Jo Jo, the Older One and yes, she breathes out hard, even Ma Z!

She looks around at the forest and takes him in too, the man of the bushes in his hand-made *'get up'*. She had often heard that as a young man and his apprenticeship at the best tailor ever, in the village, he turned out to be a very fine tailor too.

Through her tears she is sure that he has just mouthed the words *"I love you"* to her. *"I love you too, papa!"* she shouts up at the rock and wonders at the surprised look on his face. Didn't he just mouth the words *"I love you"* to her? His situation was not his fault, nothing is his fault! She curses at the Older One and runs off, sloshing along the waterlogged tracks and traces, tripping over the debris and small drowned animals.

She looks at her watch, it's seven o'clock Sunday morning ...and church! And if perchance the small village church is still standing, there would be nary a soul in attendance except for the priest and his acolytes.

She shrugs her shoulders; she had promised Dr. Brian the psychiatrist, she quickly corrects herself, *Uncle Brian* that she would be there at ten o'clock. Today the fortieth year of her being institutionalized, his mother is going home. Even though after just six months of being placed there, she was deemed capable of resuming her life on the outside, she balked. Insisting that she was not ready and would have psychotic meltdowns just before every attempt to release her.

Thereafter, she was placed in one of the rooms of the quarters, meant for the staff, because of her husband's influence and his very generous financial contributions to the institution. Now, taken in by the winsome Younger One, on her visits and the revelation by her son of how their lives intertwined, the woman insisted that she be called Mammy by the Young One.

~~~
~~~

The Young One smiles as she hops out of the taxi. She takes a deep breath and steps onto the well-manicured lawn of the small hospital that is dwarfed by the many coconut and other palm trees. The periphery of the building itself, seeming to be overwhelmed with the wide varieties of croton plants with their beautifully shaped and colorful speckled leaves that competes with the hibiscus plants and their equally beautiful hued flowers for the favorable comments of the visitors.

The Young One steps with a little hesitancy ... Yes, Mammy is going home today, home to her son's house in the city, then after some time being there, to hers at the edge of the village, which her son has lovingly maintained. The Young One had even promised her uncle Brian to eventually move in with her, *'her grandmother.'*

Mammy in turn, tried to convince the Young One that she should go to New York, to pursue her literary dreams. Then on seeing the discomfort or was it indecision on her face, Mammy, she assured the Young One that it was all for her good. She had also tried to assure her that the Older One had nothing to do with what has happened to her life and as for ***'him'***, he had already given her the most precious thing in her life, her son and that it was such a long time ago, that she can't remember his face, except that it was an ugly face. To that comment, her son the psychiatrist steupesed loudly and rolled his eyes. With a big, wicked smile plastered on her face, Mammy turned to him and broke out in the calypso *'Boo Boo man'* by the Lord Melody, referring to his father. *"Don't worry you look just like me my handsome son,"* Mammy assured him.

Now as the son pushes open the last door and nudges his mother through it, the Young One is looking at the smile slowly disappearing from off her face. The woman Mammy, steps back uncertainly; Afraid perhaps? She looks back and inhales, then exhales quickly on seeing the encouraging smile and warmth in the Young Ones eyes. She then steps out into the world that she had fled over thirty-five year ago.

Left alone, riding in the back seat of her son's car to his house in the city, Mammy's new reality begins to sink in. Waves and waves of revulsion floods her, sickening her to her stomach. Her eyes wild and dagger-like, searing into the back of the Young Ones head. Her mind full of frightening thoughts of vengeance, on Mr. Leo, Ma Jo Jo and Ma Z for foisting this new life on her, *"One! One day! She swears."*

Her fists tightly clenched, the woman Mammy, is unfeeling of her nails digging deeply into her own flesh. She's right now, oblivious to the fact that all of this, the changes, have been brought about, only because Ma Z kept the now yellowed newspaper pages; Revelations of their soiled past, that also brought the Young One into her life, her new beginning.

In the front seat with her *'Uncle Brian'*, the Young One thinks about the woman who had determinedly stalked out of the building. She had slowed and spat three times on the ground, vehemently so, as if spitting on some hated objects; People perhaps? Or perhaps a way of shedding herself of her yesterday's?

The Young One too, swears that the here and now, today, is going to be her new beginning. She will, **'must'** make it in the village, starting by helping in its rebuilding. She does not need the Older One never did, nor *'this'* Brooklyn, New York. The story of the new village would be written by her.

~~~

The man of the bushes is out of his cave-like home, which he, all by himself constructed under one of the protruding rocks along the path to the waterfall. He fashioned his home by excavating mounds of stony earth from beneath this huge rock, and then furnishing it with lots of crocus bags and flour sacks for bedding. His needs were simple, there were the spring or river whenever he needed to bathe, enough firewood from the broken branches lying under the trees from which they fell off and lots of big stones when he needed to make a makeshift fireside.

He hears it, this earth-shaking roar coming from way above his home and looks up to see the trees and tumultuous waters rushing towards his once thought of safe sanctuary. The waters effortlessly hurling him, the debris and anything else in their wake into the river below.
~~~

The man of the bushes is determined that the waters won't have there way with him as he battles the tree branches, muck and living or dead animals. The living ones doing just as he, trying to stay alive. Weak and wounded he fights the cross currents to get to the three-tier rock in the middle of the river that would most certainly blunt his fight with the raging waters. He soon gets his wish but painfully so, as he is slammed into the rock – he feels triumphant even though badly wounded. He begins to climb atop the rock, clinging onto it for dear life. The water's not letting up, still slamming into him; Beating at his head. Finally, on the second tier of the rock, the man of the river looks up questioningly at the cave above his home. He is now in a different place and time.

He sees her; The angry waters are grotesquely reshaping her sensuous lips. The lips that once kissed and caressed him; Assuring him with the words of the songs that would glide off her tongue, the words that came from deep within her soul.

He harshly breathes in, then out very, very slowly and momentarily manages to quiet his racing thoughts. She had such a beautiful voice, melodious, just like her mama's. With her songs she was able to assure him of her love, even when those voices would whisper into his ear, shout out in his head that she was about to leave him, causing him to do strange things in the village, then having the villagers either mock or fear him. Those voices that caused him to leave the beautiful home she had created, for the cave, his new home by the river, when she left him for America.

The man of the river places his hand on his throbbing head, then quickly to his ears. He doesn't need to hear the untruths about her that the river is bellowing up to him. These ugly lying words that the winds are forcing him to hear, through his fingers covering his ears; *she never did, the Older One, she lied to you, never loved you, never will!*

The man of the river is screaming out, louder and louder. The waterfall too, begins to confirm what the river and winds, just torturously bellowed to him. To everyone of his murderous screams he hears, *"she lied, she lied, she lied to you!"*

The waterfall high atop the mighty rocks, is tumbling over with an unseemly vengeance as it empties itself into the river below, its waters reaching back up to the heavens from whence it came, then bringing down the once unmovable rocks and boulders, uprooting the bamboo patches that reach way, way, down deep into the ground, as if trying to destroy the earth.

The man of the bushes is in a fight for his life, for whatever sanity that is left in his ragged soul. His screams that have become robust and bloodcurdling and resonating throughout the entire forest, have somehow quieted the roaring waterfall. Yes, she did lie to him! He would show her, he did not need her! He would now be the ruler of the forest! He would no longer be just the man of the bushes or the river, to some.

He is taken with a fresh outburst, his outraged screams are causing the broken and fallen trees to proudly rise up. The mud stuck animals to fight and release themselves from their entrapments, the river to cleanse itself from its impurities. Yes, he is now the ruler of the forest!

Doubtfully, the man of the bushes removes his hands from his ears. That voice, that cleansing voice, that oh so melodious voice, it's her the Older One! She has stopped the ugly voices in his head from repeating those equally ugly lies about her; To silence the destructive winds, their whispered lies in his ears; She is still in love with him!

Once again, the voices are beginning to rise and once again she is stepping in, stopping the seeds of doubt from taking root. Not even her being in far off New York, could destroy their love, he affirms. A tremor runs through him as his mind races back to the many times when walking through the lovers' lanes in the village, that she'd gently placed his hands on her extended belly, knowing that he was afraid too. Then she'd say it tenderly, *"feel yuh popo kick"*, repeating herself full of passion.

He lets the tears flow freely into the river, that is now churning up below him, lashing at the surrounding rocks as it stealthily creeps up his rock, to him. This he does not notice, he's thinking about their chance meeting at the river on her first visit back, after years away. He had seen her approaching him in the track. She had indeed come back to him did not leave him as the villagers said, did not send him **'totolebê,'** crazy in love. Gosh, she was breathtaking!

Then the smile on his face disappeared, when he saw the fear in her eyes. He gritted his teeth; Even with his so-called altered mind he saw that it was over. That the talk in the village about him, had gotten to her ... he had lost her.

So, what if he chose to live in the cave rather than the home they had created together, or if he chose to wear his own creations rather than the fancy things, she sent him from New York? He, giving away everything in the house that had reminders of her. Deep down he was the same Leroy her *'Roy'*. Then sadly, it became clear to him that he'd be forever looking at her day or night, through the thick bushes, as long as she was here in the village.

After their chance encounter, she never again ventured to the river, she did not want to hurt him anymore. She decided to let him be, let his heart be at rest. Instead, every night before she left for New York she would sing to him through Ma Z's open kitchen window because she knew that he would be out there, somewhere in the bushes, listening to her sing to him only, her audience of one.

She would sing to him her favorite Lena Horne songs, that her mother, Ma Jo Jo had sung to her in the past. He would sit there in the bushes on a log with his *'icy hot'* filled with his favorite bush tea and listen to his love, belting out the songs, his favorites also.

The man of the river feels the water lashing at his thighs and realizes that the waters (his tears?) were stealthily reaching up for him. He looks down at the waters that have suddenly become calm once again. He smiles; It's her. The river no longer angry, it's mouth no longer spilling out bilious refuse. Its lips once again soft, sensuous, smiling. He smiles back, yes! It's his love. Now, why are his arms no longer encircling the rock, her body? Really, why is the once angry waters now so calm and inviting and why is his body slowly sinking to nestle on its oh so placid bed?

Chapter 14

Ma Jo Jo pauses in her climb up hill to Ma Z's house, looks down into the valley and is surprised that she cannot now see the gentle and clean river and the big rocks from on which the young men would dive, pretending they were competing in the Olympics. Those river stones on which the women would wash their clothes, beating out the muck and grime from their men folk dungarees.

She looks stonily at the sea of water that has completely covered the vegetation, that has crept way up the trunks of those large and tall trees, even covering those surprisingly sturdy bearing *'paw paw trees'*, those delicious papaya bearing trees on the river's bank, that no one ever claimed to have planted.

She can still hear the scandalous laughter and cusses of the twins Myra and Mona as they gripe about their *'mingpilling'* bosses, those stingy women who expected them to serve and wait on their guests without giving them a *farthing* more. More raucous laughter would follow, after assuring each other that of course they were offered quite a few dollars more after *'giving it to them'*, their bosses, standing up to them.

She listens to the frazzled shouts of Althea threatening to *'tear up'* the behinds of her four boys, each one year apart, if they did not get out of the deep end of the river.

Now, the threatening voice of Ma Ivy calling out to Elvin and his friends, telling them that they **'better *mind'*,** be careful that none of the soot from their cooking *'land'* on her white clothes that she has been laboring behind *whole morning* on the river stones.

Ma Jo Jo looks down sadly at the frightening mass of water, knowing that she would never again or for a very long, long time, hear those Saturday morning voices. She feels happy with the knowledge that if ever she needed too, all that she had to do, was reach deep in the recesses of her mind and dredge them up; something she was quite adept at doing, as she has just done. Those voices and people not being here; just the threatening mass of water with nowhere else to go.

Ma Jo Jo on her slow and careful trek up the hill, looks on at the column of **bacchacs** with bits of green grass on their backs, as if marching to find another colony to rebuild. Some not so surefooted have fallen in the canal and swept away. The rest of the determined column marching on while more will certainly fall in, and be swept away too.

Ma Jo Jo looks around, she is sure that most of the villagers will not take that approach of staying and rebuilding like the *bacchacs*, she having recently noticed the phenomenon of some moving to the towns and cities and quite a few were joining the domestic programs and going away to Canada, England and the United States of America, most notably to Brooklyn New York.

Then too, a lot of the city and towns people seem to be in a mad rush to buy the homes of the villagers, those closer to the waterfall, fetching better prices. Some even wanting to own houses side by side. The city people sure have a lot of money the sellers would rationalize, as they'd up the prices of their homes, getting the new asking price.

With the winds whipping at them and they standing on the foundation of what was once Ma Z's house, the roof and most of the walls having collapsed, Ma Jo Jo looks at the still heavy grey clouds, she looks past the old woman standing in front of her as if pleading for her help. She who has passed through many a storm, personal and devastating ones and even managing to surmount many obstacles that they brought along, now seem no match for this one. As far as she could see, her eyes skips over the drowned vegetation. The land seeming like the very large river to the South of the country that she had only heard about, *waves* and all. Way ahead of her, through the trees still standing, many bereft of their leaves or yet still their branches, Ma Jo Jo catches the glimmer of the sun. Is the rising sun a sign letting her know that everything is going to be alright once more?

Ma Jo Jo averts her eyes once again to the woman standing in front of her with that bewildered look on her face. She is awash with pity for the woman, how helpless she seems now. The forty years of blame and guilt seem to have come down on her without a moment's notice.

Ma Jo Jo moves toward her, taking her in her arms, crushing her against her chest. Ma Jo Jo feels and hears the floodgates open as Ma Z swoons, trembles, moans and screams. The years of sorrow and guilt ending.

With tear filled eyes she looks up to the heavens and smiles, whispering a *thank you*. Never a praying person, she knows now why she had started taking to her knees since Pa Joe Joe's death – there is nothing or no one to come between the old woman and her anymore – nothing to feel guilty about.

Ma Jo Jo looks out again between the trees and is surprised that the sun has fully risen in such quick time. She sees it shining like gold dust or broken glass on the water, belying what has caused this vast sea of water to cover the land. She sighs; soon every *zandolie*, *every man jack,* would crawl out of their holes to see what the storm has wrought on the village. Yes, every creature, animal and human will be out.

Ma Z eventually frees herself from Ma Jo Jo's crushing embrace, looks up into her face as if searching for the right moment and then says wistfully. *"Happy Mother's Day Josephine."* She repeats the name over and over in her mind, Josephine! Josephine! Josephine; For forty years she dared not say the name out loud. As if startled into a reply, Ma Jo Jo stammers, *"Happy Mother's Day to you too mama."*

The two standing in the wreck of a house surveys the landscape. The water is surprisingly once again, rushing down the hill. In the far off distance, they can hear the deafening sounds of the water roaring over the waterfall and crashing on the rocks in the pool beneath.

They look at each other and nod knowingly, as a vacuum cleaner is swept by and as if guided by unseen hands, swerves and glides straight into Ma Jo Jo's steps, knocking off the remaining treaders. Pa Joe Joe had on occasions taken from the side of the road, the vacuum cleaner meant for the garbage truck and painstakingly corrected its problem, then handed it the back to the Irish woman, who would always have an astonished look on her face. The woman could never understand the anger in Pa Joe Joe's eyes or the coldness in his voice as he would lecture her about her bringing the machine from far off Ireland and dumping it without giving it a chance, trying to have it fixed.

Ma Jo Jo looks stoned faced at the vacuum cleaner and the damage that it has done to the steps. This surely is Pa Joe Joe's doing, isn't it? Ma Z shudders outwardly and clutches at Ma Jo Jo's arms, *'he isn't going to tear us apart again'* she thinks fiercely and would not relinquish her tight hold on her daughter's arms, even though Ma Jo Jo is wincing due to the pain of her fingers digging into her flesh. Ma Jo Jo leans over, her cheeks against the old woman's head. The old woman relinquishes her hold on Ma Jo Jo's arm and quickly replaces it with a hold around her waist, but this time gently so.

The both women who are being blissfully bathed with the rays of the early morning sun, look in wonder at the water running off the hill and dissipating into the earth at the foothill, where little by little patches of greenery is beginning to appear – one by one the blades of grass are beginning to pop up from beneath the mud and other debris. Yep! The sun has told them so, that all would be well again.

Gently nudging Ma Jo Jo, Ma Z enquires of her if she had heard from the Older One in New York. No! she answers dismissively with much bravado, but Ma Z had already seen the pained look on her face – before her daughter, Ma Jo Jo had pulled the veil over it.

"The Neemakharan", Ma Z bursts out forcefully. Ma Jo Jo looks down at her in astonishment, then sees the wide smile and her shaking with the laughter she is trying to suppress. Ma Jo Jo now in on the joke, says laughingly, *"no, the Neemakhran, the ungrateful one did not call."* Now they both are doubling up, laughing hysterically. This word *Neemakhran*, which they have started using, sometimes without rhyme or reason, like the rest of the villagers, they had picked up from the Indian family, the first to move into the neighborhood.

~~~

Ma Jo Jo now totally focused on her mother and with her eyes now blinded with tears of joy, did not see the sun as it gave her a conspiratorial wink of approval and the widest smile possible before it took its place in the heavens.

Back in the states, the Older One is a mixture of raw and conflicting emotions. It's already four hours since she has been trying to get in touch with her mother, Ma Jo Jo, through the Irish woman's phone, the only one in the village, but the Irish woman is not picking up or is the phone dead, she wonders. The Irish woman who would stay atop the hill and shout down hill, *"Yoo hoo! Yoo hoo! Ma Jo Jo, America is calling"*, whenever the Older One wanted some important news relayed to ma Z; Ma Jo Jo being the intermediary.

The Older One feels overwhelmed she needs her mother now, always did but was too proud to ever admit it. Mr. Leo whom she has been caring for, for twenty years, ever since he was confined to the wheelchair due to the near fatal knife wounds he suffered forty years ago back in the village, died last night. Oh, how she needs her mother now – but the Irish woman's phone just won't ring!

She really, really needs to wish her mother a Happy Mother's Day too! To tell her just how much she loves and needs her, always did too! With Pa Joe Joe gone over two weeks ago, and Mr. Leo, her father now no more, there is no one to keep them apart, ever again! This Mother's Day would be the start of their mother – daughter relationship, ***the best***, she swears fervently. Oh, if she could only reach her to wish her a Happy Mother's Day!

~ END ~
~~~